DETROIT PUBLIC LIBRARY
3 5674 00580484 5

W9-BWR-984

The Green Air

Also by David Harper

HIJACKED

BIG SATURDAY

THE GREEN AIR

A NOVEL BY DAVID HARPER

Mason & Lipscomb PUBLISHERS NEW YORK

ISBN: 0-88405-002-5

Library of Congress Catalog Card Number: 73-84877

PRINTED IN THE UNITED STATES OF AMERICA

This novel is dedicated
to three fine sailplane pilots
who risked their necks
teaching me to fly.

HOD TAYLOR
MIKE GREENWALD
STEVE BENNIS

Glider pilots in championship competition face each other and the Alaskan wilderness.

JANUARY 8:

The Visitor from Anchorage

1

"DAMMIT," the Air Force pilot yelled into his radio microphone, "I am *not* seeing things. I'm not drunk, and this is no U.F.O. It's a goddamned glider, six thousand feet above Fairbanks International. He's about two hundred yards off to my left. If you've got me on your radar, you ought to see him too."

"Negative, Air Force Three-Seven-Eight," said the cold voice of Fairbanks Tower. "Try to make closer visual contact with him."

"Beautiful!" said the Air Force pilot. "And how do you expect me to do that? He's circling at less than forty knots. This jet I'm flying falls out of the sky if I slow down under a hundred and ten. Why don't you send up one of those pokey L-16's of yours? You've got enough of them parked down there."

"Those are Air National Guard ships," said the voice from Fairbanks tower. "Besides, it's the Air Force's job to check out unidentified traffic."

"I've *checked* it out," yelled the pilot, "and like I said, it's a glider! What a minute. He's breaking off. I think he's turning into a landing pattern. My God, look at that crazy bastard! He's *slipping* that motorless mother! Now he's on his base leg, turning onto final. If you don't see him now, you'd better have the meat wagon and the headshrinkers waiting for me when I come down. If I *ever* come down."

"Well, I'll be a red-nosed reindeer," said the tower's crackling voice. "It *is* a glider!"

2

In the grace-filled sky of sailplanes, an all-wood Slingsby Skylark 12 is one of the most graceful ships there. But no one in his right mind would ever call its cockpit roomy, and therefore all six-feet-two of Barney Fields ached from almost ten hours of cramped confinement. The tall Texan pressed both feet against the rudder pedals and tried to stretch as the long runway spread out beneath him. He yawned and felt the pressure ease within his inner ears.

Barney tilted the stick and looked down one long, tapered wing as he slipped the Skylark closer to the asphalt. Then he leveled off. The ground was coming up too fast. He wanted his rollout to end near the operations building, so Barney relaxed his half-pressure on the air brake control. Immediately, the Skylark's rate of sink eased and the sailplane floated noiselessly over the runway. He dropped its nose slightly to keep the Skylark safely above the stall-out speed, and flew the plane right onto the runway, with virtually no flareout. The ship wanted to balloon, but he held it on the asphalt as the single wheel spun against the runway. His air speed indicator showed fifty-three miles an hour, against what was probably a ten mile head wind, so he was actually rolling around forty miles an hour. Barney guided the slender aircraft within fifty feet of an open hangar door and came to a stop so gentle that the tapered wings were still "flying" in the ground wind. He let one settle to the tarmac with a bump and lifted the plexiglass canopy. Shucking out of his shoulder harness, Barney disconnected his oxygen hose and carefully rolled out of the Skylark's cockpit, keeping enough weight on the ship's nose to keep its tail from dropping suddenly when his feet touched the ground. Then he grabbed the shoulder harness and pulled the sailplane's nose around so that the down wing was into the wind. He slipped out of his parachute and put it on the wing, to keep any sudden breeze from tilting it up and flipping the plane over. Only then did he turn to the amazed spectators who were gathering.

"Howdy," said Barney Fields. "Anyone got a cigarette? I ran out over Cripple Creek, and damned near had a nicotine fit."

"Cripple Creek!" one mechanic said. "Do you mean to say you came over the Alaska Range in *that* thing?"

"Good God, no," drawled Barney. "I came through the mountain passes, up the valley between Fang Peak and the Range." He accepted a cigarette, lit it, and inhaled. "Thanks. That's what I needed. All those lovely injurious tars and nicotines."

"You'd better come inside," said a uniformed official. "The operations officer is a little PO'd at you for not radioing for landing clearance."

"Sorry about that," Barney said. "My radio is out. It went blooie over Mount Russell. I was trying to gain altitude in a wave, but the roll cloud caught me and threw me around so bad that the radio came loose on its mount and broke the cables. I couldn't reach the wires in the air to reconnect them."

"Anybody who flies near Mount Russell deserves what he gets," said the first mechanic. "Those downdrafts are wicked there."

"I mean to tell you that they are," Barney agreed. "But where you hit downdrafts, you can maybe find air going up, too."

"What do you mean you tried to climb in a wave?" asked the uniformed official. "And what the hell is that roll cloud that caught you?"

"Well," Barney explained, "When a steady wind blows against a mountain range, it sets up a wave in the air, just like a wave in the water when a stream pours over a submerged rock. You've noticed those ripples that build up downstream? Waves? Well, waves in the air are the same, except they're invisible. The front side of the wave, near the mountain, is air that's going up. The back side, away from the mountain, goes down, and sets up turbulence. You can get two thousand feet a minute in a wave. Up *or* down, depending on which side of the wave you got into. Waves are what caused all those unexplained power plane crashes back in the thirties. Remember, when airliners were literally flying right into the mountains? That was because some airline pilot, fat, dumb and happy, would hit the down part of the wave and by the time that he noticed his altimeter was winding down, he'd have lost his margin of safety and would smash into the peak before he could turn away."

"And that's what he got into, the roll cloud?" asked the mechanic.

"Right. It's a big, turbulent cloud in the lee of the mountain. Nobody knew what it was until us glider boys got to fooling around with altitude flying and mapped out the wave phenomenon. The roll cloud gets its name from the way it rolls over and over. It's sudden death. There's a story about a pilot who was exploring the Bishop Wave in California. He got sucked into the roll cloud, and the next thing he knew, his glider just ripped apart. He fell out of the bottom of the cloud with the nose of the glider still attached to his shoes by the straps on the rudder pedals, and when he opened his chute, the shock pulled off both his boots. Naturally, he landed in a cactus patch."

"Mister," said the mechanic, "I think that's a lot of blue sky."

"Friend," said Barney Fields, "I speak the gospel truth, and if you doubt one word, I am sorry for you."

"Be as sorry as you want," said the mechanic. "But at least I don't go around flying in no plane without a motor."

"Amen," said the uniformed official.

3

When Barney Fields left the operations office, its chief's chewing-out still ringing in his ears, he smiled tightly.

He knew what appearance he presented. A typical "sky bum." A tall man in his late thirties, hopping around from one airport to another, picking up an occasional month's work instructing students or flying cargo.

Barney touched his left breast pocket. He wondered what the operations chief would have said if he had had X-ray vision, and could have read the figures on the certified check folded there.

$3,500,000.00.

Three and a half million dollars, folded casually and crammed into the flight suit like an old laundry list.

Just two weeks ago, he had been in Houston, Texas, dressed in a three-hundred-dollar suit from Neiman-Marcus. Across the desk from him sat a quiet, gray man with a slim leather briefcase. His name was Arnold Hobart, and he represented a Los Angeles conglomerate.

"Mr. Fields," he had said quietly, "we just don't understand you. Why do you want to take the money and run? We can't possibly pay you one-tenth of what your company is worth if you don't agree to stay with us and manage it."

"Sorry," said Barney Fields. "I'm sick of that routine. That's why I want to sell out."

Hobart consulted his notes. "According to our audit," he said, "Fields Electonics is worth, conservatively, twenty to twenty-three million dollars. Your government contracts alone will bring in nine million next quarter. But without you behind that desk, the risk is too great to pay you anywhere near market value. We'll bring in a good man, naturally, but it will take time for him to get organized."

"It won't be too tough," Barney said. "I'm leaving a fine team for him to work with. And I never did much buddy-buddy stuff with the government procurers. Their loyalty is to the company, not to me personally. As long as you deliver the merchandise, they have no reason to look around."

"Even so," Hobart said, "I don't see how we could go above three million or so. Not if you insist on leaving immediately."

"Make it three million and a half, clear," said Barney. "Wall to wall. You take everything but me, and that includes an inventory worth almost that much in itself. You pay the capital gains and other taxes, and transfer fees. Hand me a certified check for three and a half and I guarantee you, whatever your own personal commission may be, you'll make at least that much for yourself in the next fiscal year."

"Agreed," said Hobart. "But, Mr. Fields, don't you realize that if you'd only give us a year—"

"No way," said Barney.

"Six months, then. Just a hundred and eighty days. I could promise you at least five, perhaps six million—"

"I'll take the three-five today," Barney said. "Or I'll sell out to MacKay, and the only reason he wants Fields Electronics is to get my production line."

Hobart lowered his head for a moment, scribbling on a pad. He looked up. "Very well," he said. "Three million, five hundred thousand, free and clear." He shook his head. "Mr. Fields, you're cheating yourself. We want to make money, of course, but we're an ethical company—"

"I'm not cheating myself," Barney said. "Listen, Mr. Hobart, do we have a deal? Can you speak for your company?"

Hobart smiled tightly. "I can speak," he said. "In fact, while I ordinarily don't let it slip out in negotiations such as this, I *am* the company. I couldn't send a lower executive out on a deal as big as I thought this one would be."

Barney laughed. "And now that it's only a lousy three and a half million, you might just as well have sent the office boy."

"We have a deal," Hobart said. "That is, if you're sure."

"I'm sure," Barney said. He put out his hand. "Thank you, Arnie."

"I've just clipped you out of several million dollars," said Arnold Hobart. "Why are you thanking me?"

Barney Fields waved his hand toward the wide picture window overlooking the landscaped grounds around the plant. "I got out of the Air Force after Korea," he said, "and I had some pretty good ideas about aircraft instruments and guidance systems, so I figured I'd come back to Houston and set up a little shop and make a few bucks. Look what it turned into. A goddamned prison. Arnie, I own three airplanes, and every time I get behind the controls, my Board of Directors goes right into orbit. It's too risky, they say. Even the wheels over at the Manned Space Center get itchy. It's all right for Scott Carpenter to buzz around in a fighter, but let me go up to Marfa for the National Soaring Meet, and it's like I'm mailing secrets to the Russians. Who the hell needs it? I'm getting old, I'm getting smothered. I want to get out from under and find something that'll stretch my muscles. And, goddamnit, I want to *fly*! Not just on business trips with a so-called copilot, who's really there to make sure I don't hurt myself. I've been thinking of going to Alaska."

The older man's voice was surprised. "Alaska?"

"Why not? There's plenty of action there. That whole North Slope oil situation could go either way. And, Arnie, if you're a flying man, Alaska's your territory. Haven't you ever thought of just picking up and taking off like that? To somewhere where things are *happening*, not just going along business-as-usual?"

Softly, Hobart said, "Yes, I suppose I have. But I'm too old. Too locked in. If I let go for a minute, everything would collapse."

"That's what I mean," Barney said. "So who's got what? Do you have the business? Or does *it* have you?"

Hobart shrugged. "Not everyone has your freedom," he said. "I have my family to think of. My wife, my children. Even grandchildren. Perhaps if, like you, I'd never married. . . ."

Barney stared down at his hands. "I don't know," he said, finally. "Maybe, after all, you're the lucky one."

4

"Who the hell is Barney Fields?" asked Bill Webster, the mayor of Fairbanks. He was angry at being called away from his dinner. He stood in the large office he kept on the lower floor of Governor's House, glaring at Lucille Bowers, his secretary.

"A pilot from Texas," Lucille said. "He flew all the way from Anchorage to speak with you."

"What's so special about that?" Webster asked. "It's only around three hundred miles. I fly it all the time."

"In a glider?" said his secretary. "That seems a little unusual to me."

"What do you mean, a glider? Nobody's ever flown a glider through those mountains."

"Mr. Barney Fields has," Lucille said. "And he's waiting in the reception room."

"Hell," said his honor. "We're right in the middle of dinner. Give him a drink. I'll see him in half an hour."

"I've already given him a drink," she said. "He looked a little wrung-out."

"Bad flight?" Webster, an ex-Navy pilot, shared every airman's compulsion to talk about flying.

"Like you said, nobody's ever flown a glider through those mountains before."

"Bring him upstairs," Webster decided. "Amanda may kill me, but she's got a soft spot in her heart for flyboys and at least she'll feed him."

"Of course I'll feed him," said his wife, standing behind

them. "I came down to see if you two were making out on the desk. The stew's getting cold. I'm glad to see you're still the same."

Amanda Webster was one of those classic California blondes. In spite of the noxious air there, the trend seems to be toward taller and more luscious girls and, at thirty-two, Amanda was a walking endorsement of the trend. She touched her husband's waist with her hand. The gesture was warm and affectionate, but there seemed to be some final emotion missing.

Her first husband had been killed in the Anchorage earthquake of 1967. Remaining in Alaska to settle his affairs, she had met Bill Webster, who had just lost his own mate to cancer. Because both men were military pilots, although Bill was now retired, there was a kinship that immediately brought Bill and Amanda together. They found comfort in each other, and warmth. And perhaps marriage was inevitable. But the keen observer always sensed that there was some slight distance between them. The two shared respect. But love . . . ?

Seated at the dining room table, Barney Fields touched the rumpled jacket of his suit. "Sorry," he said. "The store that sold this to me said I could roll it up and the wrinkles would come right out. They lied."

"Forgot it," said Webster. "We don't stand on ceremony in this house. Or for that matter, in this state."

"This," said Amanda Webster, ladling rich, brown meat onto Barney's plate, "is the best venison stew in Alaska. Shot it myself on Thursday. You'd better take seconds, or you're in trouble."

It had been a long time since breakfast in Anchorage. Barney dug in, and Amanda smiled.

"Bill tells me you flew a glider all the way from Anchorage," she said. "I've got my own single-engine ticket, but I'd hesitate to go through those mountains even *with* a prop up front. You must have had a good wind."

"Well," Barney said, around a large chunk of fresh venison, "that isn't exactly the way a sailplane works, ma'am."

"Ma'am is short for madam," said Amanda, "and she's the old broad who runs the house up on Seward Street. I'm Amanda."

"Okay," Barney said. "Well, since you're a pilot, Amanda—"

She shook her head. "Very primitive pilot," she said. "Bill here insisted that I learn how to get one down in case he keeled over with a coronary while we were pooping around up there. That's really all I know."

Barney gave her a long look. She was deliberately underrating her knowledge. Even a single-engine ticket demands a considerable amount of training in all aspects of weather, navigation and flight performance.

"Well," he said, "like I said, a sailplane doesn't work because of the wind."

"Sailplane? I thought you came up in a glider."

Bill Webster smiled, trying not choke on his stew. He had seen Amanda put on the wide-eyed innocent act before. She was working this tall, rawboned pilot for something. Probably a demonstration ride in his glider. *Sailplane*, he corrected himself.

Barney said, "A glider is anything with wings but without a motor. But a sailplane is a super-glider. It's like the difference between an aluminum cartop boat and a racing sailboat. They both float. But the sailboat can go places and do things that aluminum boat couldn't dream of."

"Still," Amanda said, smiling, "what goes up must come down."

"Very true, ma'am," said Barney. "Amanda," he corrected.

"But whereas a glider comes down right away, with a sailplane you can cheat old Mr. Gravity for quite some time. They don't go for endurance records any more, but back in the sixties, two boys out in Hawaii stayed up for seven days and nights just to prove it could be done. We don't recognize stunts like that any more. All they prove is how long the pilots can stay awake."

"What you do," said Webster, trying to get Barney Fields off the hook, "is rise with the thermals, am I right?"

"Basically," said Barney. "The idea is to get as much height as possible out of any given upcurrent, and then scoot across the still, or maybe even falling, air as fast as possible, find another thermal, and start going up again. Now my Skylark 12, it's an English ship, sinks through still air at a given rate every second." He sipped some of the red wine Amanda had poured and smiled at her. Webster shook his head slightly. She's got him hooked, he thought.

"But you're not sinking all the time," said Amanda. "Sometimes you're rising, isn't that what you said?"

"Let me take it a step at a time," Barney said. "My rate of sink is two feet a second. That means that every second I'm in the air, I will sink two feet. Or a hundred and twenty feet a minute. With me so far?"

Amanda smiled over her wine glass. "All the way," she said.

"Okay. Now, what happens if instead of being in still air, I'm flying in *rising* air? Say it's rising at a rate of ten feet a second."

"Do you mean rising like smoke from a chimney?" she said.

"Yes. Warm air, like smoke, rises. Of course, you can see the smoke, and most of the time, you can't see thermals. Thermals, you might remember that from your flight training, they're bubbles of air warmer than the surrounding atmosphere, so they go up just like smoke until their heat has been absorbed by the surrounding air."

"Aha!" cried Amanda. "The rising air gets under your wings and pushes you up?"

Barney shook his head. "It's not a push. Remember, I'm in that mass of air. I'm falling through it at two feet a second. But it's going up at ten feet a second. So even though I'm going down at two feet a second, within my air mass, my total gain of altitude will be eight feet a second. And as long as my bubble of air is rising faster than my own rate of sink, I'll go up with it. When it poops out, I strike off looking for another bubble. They're like invisible elevators in the sky."

"Have some more stew," said Bill Webster.

Barney pushed back his chair. "Many thanks," he said. "But I think I just increased my rate of sink by another foot per second."

Amanda laughed. "Come into the study," she said. "There's a fire and some good brandy."

Stretched before the fireplace, Barney sipped from a snifter and sighed. "Would you believe that two weeks ago I was in Houston, Texas, chug-a-lugging Mexicali beer and wondering what Alaska was like? Now I know. It's warm fireplaces and old brandy and beautiful wives of mayors."

Bill Webster sipped his own brandy. "The frontier days are going," he said. "When I first got here, nine years ago, you couldn't find a decent bottle of brandy. But air cargo changed that. This comes directly from France. It doesn't even go through the South Forty-Eight."

"South Forty-Eight?"

"That's what we call you folks down there. Our friends in Texas have never forgiven us. Because the Lone Star is only Number Two, now, in size."

"That doesn't bother me," said Barney. "I was born in New Jersey, anyway."

"Where are you staying in Fairbanks?" asked Amanda.

Barney shrugged. "I'll find a motel. I changed at the airport and picked up a rental car, but it was getting late and I wanted to get over here and see the mayor as soon as I could."

Amanda laughed. "You're absolutely out of your mind. Where do you think you'll find a motel room without a reservation? I think you'd better stay with us."

"I couldn't put you to that bother. You've been too kind already, seeing me without an appointment and feeding me and—"

Webster spoke up. "Amanda's right. This town is tight for rooms. We've got the biggest housing shortage in the hemisphere. And we've got plenty of room here. The last mayor had six kids. We don't have any, and those rooms are just eating up heat. We might as well get our money's worth out of them."

He got up. "I'll get the housekeeper to set a room up for you. Dear, why don't you show Mr. Fields where to plug his car in?"

"Plug my what?"

"Follow me," said Amanda Webster. Barney trailed her outside, into the dry bitterness of the cold evening. "You should have plugged it in when you arrived."

"Amanda," said the pilot, laughing, "I don't know what the hell you're talking about."

"You will, the first time you find your crankcase frozen solid and can't get your car started."

He shrugged, following her down the icy sidewalk. "I assumed a rental car would have antifreeze in the radiator."

"It does. It's your oil you have to worry about. Is this Chevy yours?"

"It belongs to Hertz, but they let me have it in exchange for my American Express card."

"Well, pull out that little plug there, under the hood."

Barney bent over. There *was* a cord, like one end of a lamp's, with two metal prongs.

She showed him a metal electrical junction box mounted on top of a pole, like a parking meter. "Plug it in here. There's an electric crankcase heater in your engine. This will keep it from freezing overnight and you'll be able to start in the morning."

Barney shook his head. "I'll be goddamned," he said. Then, "Sorry."

Amanda tilted her head. "Why?"

"My language is a little rough sometimes." He spread his hands. "I don't want to offend you."

"You don't," she said. "I'm an Army brat. My first husband was military. Bill's Navy. I knew what all the words meant by the time I was ten."

They started back into the house. It was a sprawling frame building, with numerous gables and very steep roof surfaces. Water dripped from all the eaves.

Amanda saw him looking at the spattering drops. "Yes," she said, "I know it's well below freezing. We have heating elements on the eaves, to keep ice from building up. Otherwise, the weight could pull off the gutters."

"What do you do if the electricity fails?"

She closed both her hands. "Sometimes I wonder myself. We're all too dependent on it. If the generators run out of fuel, or all break down at once . . . or if some enemy takes them out, I think we'd be in real trouble."

She turned toward the entrance. He caught her shoulder.

"What?" she said, turning back.

"Amanda . . . what are you up to? If you've got your

license, you have to know more about soaring than you're letting on. Hell, I know guys who even go soaring in their Piper J-3's, just shut the engines off and treat the plane like a glider. Why are you pretending that it's all new to you?"

She smiled. "Because, my wild blue yonder friend, you want something from my husband, and it depends on his understanding what you're talking about. Bill's an old jet pilot. Those birds glide just like bricks. A flameout and you're in the drink in two minutes. So I thought I'd play audience, and let him hear what you have to peddle."

"Why?"

Her eyes met his. "Why not?"

Their gaze remained locked for what seemed a very long time. "Why not?" Barney repeated, and followed her inside.

Bill Webster was adding another log to the fire. "It's getting cold," he said. "You're all set, Barney. Head of the stairs and turn right."

"Great," said Barney, settling down with his brandy again.

"We're making our own thermals tonight," said Amanda.

Her husband looked at her. "What?"

"With the fireplace," she said calmly.

Bill Webster lit a cigar, after offering one to Barney, who refused.

"How high do thermals go, anyway?" he asked Barney. "I suppose I've hit them, but those stove pipes I flew were so heavy, it took a real tough clout of clear air turbulence to even shake the wings."

"It all depends," Barney said, glancing at Amanda, who was smiling slightly as she stared at the fire. "Most thermals condense into cumulus clouds. They're those white, fluffy ones you see on a hot day. Their height above terrain depends on the amount of moisture in the air, the temperature, and so on. Most times, you can find a thermal and take it up four, five thousand feet before you reach cloud base. That's where the moisture in the thermal starts condensing and forming the cloud. In this country, you would have to break off your flight there, because if you're in a controlled flight zone, you aren't allowed to fly in clouds on instruments. In Europe, it's different, and the pilot can go right up inside the cloud, all the way to its top. If it's a cumulonimbus, a thunder cloud, it might get him up to fifteen thousand feet or so." Barney sipped his brandy. "But you don't have so many control zones here in Alaska. I think this may be just about the most promising soaring country in the world."

"Why do you say that?"

"You need several factors for good soaring. First, you have to get what we call an unstable air mass. Power pilots hate them, because all the ups and downs mean turbulence and a rough flight. But the soaring pilot loves turbulence. Next, you need plenty of safe places to land, because you can't always go where *you* want to go. I don't mean to tell you about your own state, Mr. Mayor–"

Webster waved a hand. "It's Bill."

"Bill. But Alaska has more landing strips than any state in the Union. At last count, more than five hundred."

"It's the only way we can get around," said Webster. "There simply aren't any roads through most of the state. We travel by water or air or not at all."

"Just my point," said Barney Fields. "Next, having all your mountains doesn't hurt a bit. Those peaks can put up a standing wave under the right wind conditions, and a good wave could mean a try for the world's altitude record. Add up all of these things and you see that Alaska's a great place to fly. But I haven't even mentioned the most important factor."

"Which is?"

"Bill, you can only keep your sailplane in the air as long as warm air is rising off the ground and floating up into colder air above. It takes the sun to warm that ground air. *How* warm doesn't matter just so long as it's warmer than the surrounding air. So the limit to how long and how far you can fly is determined by the hours of sunlight you have."

"That sounds reasonable."

Barney leaned forward. "How many hours of sunlight does Fairbanks have in July?"

"Every kid knows that. More than twenty. We have midnight baseball games without lights."

"That's right, Bill. Twenty hours of sunlight. More than double what we get in most places. That means at least sixteen hours of useful flying conditions, opposed to eight or nine down in the South Forty-Eight. Now, don't quote me on the names and world's records I'm going to give you next, because they keep changing, but the last time I looked, the world's distance record for a sailplane was held by Alvin Parker, of good old Texas, for flying 646 miles."

Bill Webster whistled. Barney continued. "For altitude, Paul Bikle of the U.S.A. gained 42,303 feet in the Bishop Wave. His true altitude was more than forty-six thousand feet. And that was years ago. Paul was flying an all-metal Schweizer 1-23E, back in 1961. Anyway, I guess you see what I mean. To a sailplane pilot, breaking records is a serious business. We'll go anywhere, pay anything, and suffer any inconvenience for a shot at a new one. Bill, I'm convinced that with the right kind of luck, soaring pilots could come up here to Alaska, wipe that record slate clean, and start over."

Amanda Webster sat back slowly, her eyes shining. She stared at Barney Fields.

"It sounds fascinating," said her husband. "But why did you come to me?"

"Because you're a pilot. You could talk to the governor."

"About what?"

"Oh?" said Barney. "Didn't I mention it? I think that Alaska ought to make a bid for this year's World Soaring Championships."

5

"He sounds like a member of a rare breed," said the governor of Alaska. He and Mayor Bill Webster were seated in the Baranof Hotel, Juneau's popular luncheon spot. "It sounds as if he's convinced you, Bill."

"He has. Will you talk to him?"

The governor spread his hands. "Of course. But to what end? Bill, we've got our own problems. This whole North Slope oil business has hurt our image world-wide. One faction yells we stole it from the Indians. The conservationists scream we're going to melt the permafrost and destroy the caribou herds. The oil companies are crying foul, that we misled them into investing billions of dollars in oil fields that can't be exploited. To be coldly realistic, what's in this soaring meet for us?"

"I knew you'd ask that. I asked it myself. I think an event of this nature can dramatize the pioneer spirit of our state. We'll get world-wide coverage. I called an old buddy of mine down at ABC television. He thinks *Wide World of Sports* would be very interested. In the long run, tourism may be better for our economy than oil wells. Let's show the world that we've got more than the northern lights and glaciers."

The governor sipped his martini. "You may be right, Bill. It's no secret that I hesitate to tie our coattails to any one industry. I suppose it'd do no harm to talk to your young man. The next time I come up to Fairbanks—"

"I'll bring him in. He's outside, in the bar."

The governor of Alaska looked at Bill Webster carefully. "You were very sure of me, weren't you?"

"Yes sir, I was," said Bill.

When Barney Fields came in he was greeted warmly by the governor. Bill ordered a round of drinks, and then the governor said, "You look like a young man who knows the answers."

"Try me," said Barney.

"What would this soaring meet cost us?"

"Practically nothing." The governor snorted, and Barney went on. "No sir, I'm not giving you a snow job. Let me tell you what's involved, and see if you agree. This isn't like bidding on an Olympics and having to put millions into construction and facilities. Let's start with the way the soaring teams are made up. You'll have, at the most, twenty nations involved. Perhaps ten men per nation. That's only two hundred men or so."

"How do the teams break down?" asked the governor. "You're not going to have two hundred planes involved, are you?"

Barney laughed. "No sir. Probably around eighty. Two pilots from each country will be in Open Class. That's the class for ships with wing spans wider than sixty feet. And two in Standard Class, for ships with spans under sixty feet."

"Listen to what comes next," Bill Webster urged. "It's amazing."

"I suppose what the mayor means," said Barney, "is that

in most cases, the individual pilot provides his own aircraft. The only exceptions are usually from Iron Curtain countries who subsidize their pilots pretty heavily."

"Then except for those countries," said the governor, "it's a rich man's sport."

Barney shook his head. "Not at all. A high-performance sailplane can cost six, seven thousand dollars. But so does a high-performance car." He grinned. "Most pilots drive old heaps. They put their money in the air."

"Still," the governor persisted, "it costs real money to gallivant around the world to competitions."

"True," said Barney. "But we get help. In the U.S., individuals and industry chip in. There's no hiding it, the costs *are* high. You've got entrance fees, they could be four, five hundred dollars a pilot. And transportation, meals, not to mention hidden costs such as gasoline for the retrieving team."

The governor put down his drink. "What on earth is a retrieving team?"

"Well," said Barney, "A sailplane may land two or three hundred miles away from the home field. The retrieving team is a crew which has been chasing the sailplane during its flight. It's usually a car or truck with a special trailer. They keep in touch by sight, or radio, or sometimes by plain luck. When the plane lands and the retrievers catch up with it, they take the ship apart, pack it on the trailer, and drive all night to get back to the field in time for the next day's flight."

"I'll be goddamned," said the governor. "And I suppose the pilot gets his beauty rest in the back seat of the car?"

"That's the idea," said Barney.

The governor attacked his drink. "Mad," he said. "You're all stark raving mad."

"You won't get any argument from me about that," said Barney, laughing.

"Well," said the governor, "that's the end of it. There's no way to have your sailplane meet up here."

Bill Webster asked, "Why not?"

"No roads, Bill. This isn't Kansas, you know."

Barney leaned forward. "I realize that, sir," he said. "And the retrieve problem stumped me when I first started thinking of this area. I studied the maps, and you're right. A sailplane down at the strip at Fort Yukon, for instance, even in summer, could never get out by road. I thought of floating down the rivers, but that would be too slow."

"That's what I mean," said the governor. "And if what I understand about soaring is right, you couldn't limit your flights to those areas with good roads."

Glumly, Bill Webster said, "I didn't think of this, Barney. What good is it to have twenty hours of sunlight if you can't get the ships home after each flight?" He gulped his own drink. "Parkinson's Law, or is it Murphy's? If something *can* go wrong, it *will*. I don't see any way around it."

"How about *over* it?" said Barney, grinning.

"What do you mean, over?"

"Who says we have to retrieve with cars and trailers just because that's the way it's always been done before?"

Bill Webster started to answer, and the governor cut him off. "What other way is there, Mr. Fields?"

"Tow planes."

"You mean tie the gliders behind a regular airplane?"

"Why not? That's the way they get airborne in the first place, attached to an aerial tug. Why not do away with the old-fashioned trailer retrieve? Instead of each pilot having a couple of frustrated buddies tooling along on the ground in a fast car, he'll have a tow plane assigned to him from the beginning of each flight to its conclusion. We'll furnish a tow plane and a tow pilot. The team will furnish a backup glider pilot to fly the glider back on tow. Let's say our man goes down at Fort Yukon, as we discussed. A couple of minutes after he lands, the tow plane will show up, because it's been tracking him all along his flight. It lands, the backup pilot gets in the glider, the regular pilot gets in the tow plane, and snoozes happily away back to Fairbanks."

The governor pulled at his moustache. "It might work," he admitted. "But what happens if the sailplane goes down in the bush instead of that Fort Yukon strip?"

"I've talked with the boys at the Air National Guard. They say their new L-16's will land and take off anywhere a glider could have gotten down safely. And for that one place in a thousand where a glider goes into an area where an L-16 can't land, we'll do a snatch pickup. The tow plane will drop two aluminum poles along with a special tow rope. The pilot sticks the poles in the ground with the rope between them, and the tow plane snatches the glider up into the air with a hook as it flies over. I've seen this technique work. It's even been used to pick up men in special parachute harnesses."

The governor looked at Barney, then at Bill Webster. "My congratulations," he said. "Your pilot friend seems to have this all well thought out."

Bill leaned forward. "Does that mean you're with us?"

"I think so."

"How many planes did you say to expect?"

"At the most, eighty," said Barney.

"Eighty! Where will we get eighty L-16's?"

"You've already got them," said Barney. "Your Air National Guard unit at Fairbanks has more than a hundred. This whole affair can be a training exercise for your Guard pilots. You've already got that allocated in your budget. I know. I checked."

"Such deviousness delights me," said the governor. "By the time you get through, I wouldn't be surprised if the venture shows a profit."

"I doubt that," said Barney. "But your only expenses will be for food and other support operations that the Guard couldn't be expected to pick up. I'm hoping each nation's private air carriers can be persuaded to get the ships to Fairbanks. From there on, the Air National Guard will take over."

"Assuming I say go ahead, what's your next move?"

Barney spread a sheaf of credentials on the table. "I'm already lined up with the Soaring Society of America, in California. They agree that Alaska would be an ideal site. You see, the original meet this year was scheduled to be held in Poland, and because of the rebellion there last month, the meet was cancelled. I think we should put in a bid to the FAI, that's the Fédération Aeronautique in France. They handle all world records and competitions in aeronautics. We'd have a good chance. Because the timing's so tight, they may not be able to come up with another site otherwise."

"Convenient," said the governor.

"No sir," said Barney. "The trouble in Poland is what gave me the idea. I went to the SSA, and they said to come on up and talk to you. Otherwise, there may not be a meet this year."

"If it goes through," the governor mused, "I suppose it would be wise to appoint you head of operations."

"Not on your life," said Barney. "I'm flying. But the SSA will give you a good man. And the chief of the Air National Guard will be able to take care of the logistics of the L-16s and the base facilities. Someone'll have to clear possible flights into Canada, especially into the Yukon territory, since some of the distance runs might be made in that direction. But whatever we do, we'd better do it right now, because July isn't that far off."

The governor pushed his glass away. "All right," he said. "I'm convinced. I'll get this thing into formal committee and so on. But don't worry, it'll pass. So you'd better have your Soaring Society get in touch with that FAI French outfit."

"I'm on my way," said Barney, getting up. He shook the hands of both the governor and Bill Webster. "I'll get right on the phone."

"See you in a few minutes, Barney," said Webster, as the pilot left.

"I may be up Fairbanks way next week," said the governor. "Do you think your young Mr. Fields might be around?"

"I think so," said Webster. "He's staying with us."

"What does he do in the line of work?"

Webster made a puzzled expression. "You know," he said slowly, "I don't have the faintest idea."

"He's too good a man to be idle," said the governor. "If he's looking for a job, maybe we can come up with something."

"I'll check into it."

"Fine. Meanwhile, if he's got time, I might persuade him to give me a glider ride. You know, Bill, I've been flying for more than thirty years, and until this moment, I've never been remotely tempted to go up without an engine in front of me. Do you think I'm finally entering my second childhood?"

"Well, sir, if you are, you're in good company. Barney took Amanda for her first ride yesterday."

6

The news that the state of Alaska had been chosen for the year's Internationals was flashed around the world within hours. Pilots who had been reexamining their flight schedules with disappointment began calling libraries and newspapers for information about Alaska, its weather and terrain.

In Poland, Jan Makula put the nose of his Foka 14 into a steep dive and watched the airspeed indicator's needle creep upward, toward the red line marking danger. Then, as he applied the enormous spoilers and dive brakes, he felt the slim aircraft slow. The needle trembled down into the safety zone again. Makula smiled. The effectiveness of these speed-limiting devices would give his team a strong advantage in the turbulent cloud conditions he expected to encounter in Alaska.

In West Germany, Wolf Lindner floated his all-wood Ka-20 toward an ominous hedgerow that crouched between him and the safety of a plowed field. His strategy for Alaska would be to stretch his final glide to its ultimate, and his practice session today had left him over unfriendly forest. Even by applying the best possible lift-over-drag speed, it seemed likely that he might land on top of that forbidding hedge. But Wolf had one trick left. He shoved the control stick forward and the Ka-20 dove toward the bottom of the hedge. Air speed built up. Near the ground now, Wolf was doing more than ninety miles an hour. As the hedge loomed up before him, he pulled the stick back into his stomach. The sailplane ballooned up into the air, trembling near the stall, floated over the hedgerow with feet to spare, and settled down easily in the soft earth.

Over the brightly checkerboarded fields of Basingstoke, England, Chet Cameron inhaled the cool air and spiraled toward a towering cumulonimbus in his Dart 27. The afternoon was well under way, and the clouds would begin deteriorating before long. But not, Chet hoped, before he had made one more try for the Altitude Diamond on his Gold "C" badge. Other fliers had advised him he was sure to get that diamond in Alaska, but Chet was still uneasy about the meet's new locale and doubted that it would ever come off. Behind him, he could hear the two sealed barographs ticking away, each marking its official version of every minute and the altitude achieved during it. He tilted his head and peered at the great thunderhead. It seemed to stretch up almost out of sight. With luck, he would be able to enter without too much bouncing around and spiral up through rain and thunder, then ice and hail, and emerge from its domed crown at a total gain of more altitude than he would need for the cherished diamond. To win it, he had to gain 16,400 feet. Chet slipped his oxygen mask over his guardsman moustache and tasted the moldy rubber of the mouthpiece. He took a last look around at the sunlit world, and the Dart 27 spiraled up into the swirling mists.

In the lee of the Soviet Ural Mountains, Major Anton Suslov put his late model KAI-26 through its paces. Since he had become the first Russian cosmonaut to walk on the moon, the Russian authorities had been more friendly toward Suslov's frequent participation in foreign soaring competitions. Suslov had just finished checking the stall speed of the improved KAI, and while he felt that its level of forty-one miles an hour was still excessive, it was within bounds. He was disappointed to learn that Alaska had been chosen as the site for the meet rather than New Zealand, and tried to remember what little he knew of Alaskan geography. Only a gigantic wave condition such as the Bishop Wave in California, or the magnificent Northwest Arch over Christchurch, New Zealand, would give him a chance of beating the American Paul Bikle's record of 46,267 feet absolute altitude. Some pilots claimed that Bikle's feat was the limit—in fact, *beyond* the limit—to which a man might fly with only pure oxygen and an unpressurized cabin. Suslov was unconvinced. If one man could live to 46,267 feet, another might survive at forty-seven thousand. Or would that be enough? Hadn't he heard that the new international rules made a three percent increase over the previous record necessary? In that case, he would need a total altitude of 47,655 feet. Forty-eight thousand even, to be safe. Could he do that in Alaska? Major Anton Suslov, who once walked in the Sea of Tranquility at Moon Base One, was not at all sure.

Near Paris, her short blonde hair streaming back in the slipstream, Renée Duval slipped out of her shoulder harness and rolled from the wildly tumbling Edelweiss sailplane, four thousand feet over the plains of France. Her face was flushed more from anger than fear. This airplane would have brought her victory in Alaska, just as it had in two previous world championships. And now, as she had been practicing spin recovery, a sudden cracking sound had announced the collapse of the twin "V" tail. Unknown to her, a student pilot had damaged it with a bad landing and had not reported his mistake. Renée's parachute opened and, with enormous sadness, she watched the crippled plane flutter toward the yellow fields below.

Six thousand feet over Fairbanks, Barney Fields lifted both hands in the air and said to his new student, Amanda Webster, "Okay, honey. You're flying this bird."

As the graceful two-place Schweizer 2-32 mushed around the sky under the inexperienced hands of her new pilot, Barney leaned back against his parachute. By God, he thought, I'm going to pull it off. He had been involved in secret negotiations with a major oil company, and there was a very good chance that he would parlay his three and a half million dollars into ten times that by setting up a charter service to the North Slope. But, more important at this moment, the international meet was coming to Alaska in July, and under the impetus of competition flying, Barney was determined to get that distance record of a thousand miles. Only in Alaska, with its wealth of thermals, would it be possible.

"Green air," he mumbled. "Goddamnit, feel that green air."

"What's green air?" asked Amanda Webster.

"Huh?"

"You just said, 'green air.' What does that mean, Barney?"

"Oh." Barney shook his head, bringing himself back to the present and this cockpit. "See that little doohickey on the instrument panel? That's our backup variometer. We've got the regular dial one, but this is the old Cosim Variometer. Us humans, we're not as sensitive as birds, so we need an instrument to let us know whether we're going up or going down. See those two tubes—the one with the red pellet shows you when you're in sinking air. You don't want that. The other one, with the green pellet, shows you when you're in air that's rising. That's what we want. So when the green pellet goes up in its tube, we're in 'green air.' Green air's what every soaring pilot searches for all his life. And, baby, this state of Alaska is really and truly the land of green air."

The sailplane trembled as one wing made a booming sound and leaped upwards. Barney yelled, "Feel that? It's a boomer! Turn! Turn into it. And look at the variometer!"

Amanda shouted, "It's green!"

"Taste it!" said Barney Fields. "Taste that green air!"

JUNE 24: *The Practice Week*

1

THE long shadows of the midnight sun slanted across the wide runways of Eielson Air Force Base, southeast of Fairbanks along the southern edge of Moose Creek. Sixty-seven sailplanes were lined up in untidy rows along the seven-thousand-foot auxiliary strip which had been assigned for use by the competition. A sixty-eighth plane, lately arrived, was half-assembled in a nearby hangar. Seventeen nations had entered the meet, and most of their personnel had already arrived.

Jake Huggins, editor of the Fairbanks *Eagle*, had already interviewed most of them. To his secretary, who had the unpleasant task of typing his scrawled notes into readable English, he muttered several times, "They're nuts. Every damned one of them. Loony bin material."

To the casual observer, Jake might have appeared to be a typical latter-day sourdough. His rough clothing and the three days of beard that always roughed his face made him look more like a miner fresh from the creek than a former managing editor of the New York *Daily News* and two-time winner of the Sigma Delta Chi award. One morning, Jake got up from his desk, strolled out as if going for coffee, and never came back. A year later he turned up in Alaska, much thinner, tanned, and bought the *Eagle*, a failing county weekly. Now the *Eagle* was healthy, published three times a week, and Jake was muttering about big-city pressures again and threatening to go back in the bush with a mimeograph machine and start up the Point Barrow *Icicle*.

"How did all this gliding business start, anyway?" he asked Ron Smith, his guest for lunch at the Northern Lights Club. Smith was the official taskmaster for the competition. Sixty-three and balding, Ron Smith had twice been president of the Soaring Society of America, and held the third Diamond "C" badge ever issued. With Smith and Huggins was Ben Wade, a cameraman for ABC's *Wide World of Sports*. A stocky, silent man, he studied the faces of the two men across the table, observing the play of light and shadow across them.

"That was a long time before the Wright brothers," said Ron Smith. "In 1855, to be precise. A Frenchman was towed off in his homemade glider by horse power. The flight wasn't very long, but it was the first recorded. I'm not deprecating the Wrights, of course. Orville Wright flew a glider at Kitty Hawk in 1911 for nine minutes and forty-five seconds. That record held up for years to come. But Orville didn't stop there. He and his brother put an engine in the plane and began the horsepower race. Now the sky is full of jets and they're talking of limiting gliders to little enclaves."

"I still don't know what keeps them up," said Jake.

"World history would be different today if it weren't for gliders," Smith went on. "Without gliders, Hitler never would have had a Luftwaffe, and without the Luftwaffe, there would have been no World War II. It was even a German who first discovered thermals, during the first glider contest ever held. In the Rhone Mountains, 1920. His name was Wolfgang Klemperer."

"But what keeps them up?"

"In fact, most of the basic aerodynamic principles we use today were developed by the Germans, at the Technical High School of Hanover. They built the first true sailplane."

"I still want to know what keeps them up," Jake said.

Ron Smith smiled suddenly, looking astoundingly like a flight-jacketed pixie. "I'd think you newspaper people would be very familiar with what keeps them up, Jake."

Suspiciously, Jake asked, "What?"

Smith sipped his scotch and water. "Hot air. Plenty of hot air."

2

One end of a heated hangar had been filled with chairs facing a long table and a series of maps and blackboards. The competitors sat in the chairs and the officials were gathered around the table.

Ron Smith was at the blackboard, chalk in hand. He had just finished printing a list of tasks.

"We'll put this through the mimeo this evening," he told the pilots. "But I thought you might like to know what the tasks will be as soon as possible." He looked around at the tense faces. How young, Ron thought. Then, sadly, no . . . not so young at all. It's just that I'm so old.

"This week, as scheduled, is for practice. Get used to the runway, the approaches. You'll find thermal activity up here very different from that you're used to. It builds slowly in the morning, gets pretty bumpy during midday, and then gives you a long, gentle period for quite some time in the late afternoon and evening. The activity then will be either zero sink or very mild green air."

Barney Fields sat in the front row. He was absent without leave from a meeting he had scheduled up north with the oil company, but the glow of having made the American competition team still flushed his thin face. It had been real luck having two of the American fliers who would certainly have bumped him off the team run into personal difficulties that kept them from coming to Alaska. Wally Scott was out because of illness, and Dick Schreder had flown his newly-constructed HP-24 into a virtually invisible power cable in the Arizona desert and was laid up with a broken leg.

"As you see," said Smith, "on July 1, we'll have the opening ceremonies. There might even be a drink or two."

His audience laughed. "But not more than two. Because July 2, we've got a lovely 306-mile triangle for you." The pilots groaned. "It won't be as bad as you think. Remember you'll have more than sixteen flying hours if the thermals start popping early. One thing you won't have to worry about is rain. Quite the opposite." He nodded at an Air Force officer seated at the table. "Colonel?"

The officer stood. "Good morning. I'm Colonel Harvey Jenkins, and I'm weather officer here at Eielson." He indicated a weather map. "As you can see from the isobars, everything looks fine on the long-range projection. The Japanese air currents are flowing off the tip of Attu Island where they belong, and there's a nice frontal system moving up from the Bristol Bay area. Good soaring conditions." He made a heavy crayon mark that bisected the state. "But if this happens, if those Jap currents swing northeast, we might get an inversion that could last for days. That'd give us nice calm skies . . . perfect for power pilots, but I gather you boys would hope for more unstable conditions."

"Not half right," called Chet Cameron. The English pilot was standing near the rear of the crowd, his chubby figure leaning against the partially dismantled fuselage of a jet fighter. "What we want are real stinko skies."

The officer laughed. "Well, I'm sure you can count on convection for the rest of this week." He indicated a series of markings near the top of the map. "Then, if the Jap currents stay down where they belong and this cold air mass starts moving in from the Arctic Ocean, you ought to have enough convection to fly a barn door."

Seated well in the back, Jake Huggins turned to a neighboring pilot and hissed, "What the hell's convection?"

Major Anton Suslov, the Soviet pilot, said, "Convection is instability or vertical movement of the air. It is necessary to keep our sailplane aloft. If we suffer an inversion, such as is so common in your Los Angeles, the air below would be trapped by a heavier upper layer, and thermal activity would be severely limited."

The newspaperman stared at the Soviet cosmonaut. "Thanks," he said dryly. "I'm sorry I asked."

"Got it on the weather?" asked Ron Smith. "Okay, the next task will be one you boys—" he nodded toward Renée Duval, the French pilot, —"*and* girls love. A race." He pointed at the map. "All the way up to Point Barrow. Five hundred and two miles. Of course, if the wind isn't right for the attempt, the committee will come up with another task. But our estimate now is that many of you should make the goal. And for those of you who are interested, you'll remember that distance is more than enough for your distance and goal diamonds."

The pilots applauded. This was turning out to be a different kind of meet. Too often the competitions were just that; struggles between individual pilots and teams without leaving room for attempts at the coveted gold and diamond awards.

"You'll have a rest day, of course," Smith went on. "Then for anyone who might have an eye on that distance record, we're going to have a Free Distance Day."

This time the pilots actually stood up and cheered. Ron Smith waved his arms. "Hold it down! Wait until you get a good look at that terrain out there, and then decide if we're doing you any favors." He looked around. "Any questions?"

Renée Duval stood. "Can you tell me the reason for the new equipment that is being mounted in our sailplanes? We all already have excellent radio equipment."

A second Air Force officer stood. "I'll answer that, ma'am. I'm Captain Tim Sanders, and I'm in charge of the tow and retrieve operation. As you know, we'll be working with aero retrieves here. Well, we found in our first practice flights that it isn't as easy as we thought to keep a sailplane within sight of an L-16. It's wasteful of gas and manpower to try to fly alongside the sailplane, not to mention distracting and possibly dangerous. So we're going to use the equipment we're installing now, long-range transponders. Each transponder will pinpoint the sailplane's exact location and identity. Instead of trying to follow you, your tug will be somewhere within an hour's flight, and when you go down, you radio for a pickup."

"What if we have radio failure?"

"No problem, ma'am. The fact that your transponder signal isn't moving will tell us you're on the ground."

"Suppose our signal is blocked by the mountains?" asked Wolf Lindner.

"No way, sir. We have communications centers at all four

points of the compass. Plus an Air Force radar plane orbiting at fifty thousand feet. He can scan most of the state. It's not likely you'll get out of range."

"Unless," Major Anton Suslov said quietly, "one should climb one's sailplane *above* fifty thousand feet."

"Well, yes," said Captain Tim Sanders, "That might cause some problems. But I doubt that will happen."

"If the cold front moves in from the Arctic," said Suslov, "and strikes the Alaska Range, a high standing wave might occur, particularly in the lee of Mount McKinley. Is that not so?"

Sanders looked at Colonel Jenkins, the weather officer. "It's possible," said Jenkins.

"So," said the Russian. "We shall see."

Ron Smith stood up again. "Any more questions?" No one answered. "All right, we've got a little practice mission today for those who want it and have their ships ready." He indicated the large scale map. "A three-hundred-kilometer triangle. Turn points are at Nenana and at the Bonnifield airstrip, south of Fairbanks. It's a milk run. The thermals are popping out there, and you'll never be too far from a safe landing strip." He looked at his watch. "It's 0915 now. Take off any time after ten hundred hours. Check in with Captain Jenkins to see if your transponders are installed yet."

When he spoke to the Air Force officer, Barney Fields found that his had not been. "Sorry, Mr. Fields," said Jenkins. "I didn't know you were going to fly today."

"Don't sweat it," said Barney. "I'll just go up and poke around with the Schweizer."

"Do you want a chase plane anyway?"

"No. If I come down off a strip, I'll radio you."

"Roger."

Barney went to the other side of the hangar where the

coffee machine was. Bill and Amanda Webster were there. Bill handed him a cup of black coffee.

"Thanks," said Barney. "My Skylark isn't ready, so I'm going to take the Schweizer. There's an extra seat, Bill. Want to go for a ride?"

The Mayor laughed. "Like hell," he said. "You're not going to get me up in a crate that doesn't have either a coffee mill in front or a stove pipe behind."

"You don't know what you're missing," Barney said. "I know a lot of jet jockeys who enjoy soaring."

"Why don't you go, Amanda?" said Webster.

She looked at her husband, then at Barney. "I really ought to see after those two lady reporters who are coming in from Los Angeles."

"I'll take care of the ladies of the press," said her husband. "You've been working too hard. Go ahead, enjoy yourself. Maybe Barney will even let you get in an hour of flight time."

Amanda looked at the tall Texan. "Do you mind?"

"Mind? I'm delighted."

Amanda kissed Bill Webster on the cheek. "See you later, dear."

"Have fun," he said.

As they walked out to the flight line, Amanda asked Barney, "Where did you go yesterday?"

"Up to the oil camp."

She hesitated. "Oh? Are you looking for a job?"

Thinking of the three and a half million dollars in his account at Fairbanks Trust, Barney smiled. "No," he said.

"That's good," Amanda answered. "Because it might not have lasted too long."

"Don't you like oil wells?"

"I don't like anything that could turn this state into a northern version of Texas." Amanda stopped. "Oh! Barney, I didn't–"

"Don't worry," he said. "I don't particularly appreciate what the oil people have done to Texas, either."

"Let's change the subject. If today's flight were a real competition, how could they tell that you'd really been where you said?"

"There're a couple of ways. They could issue you a sealed camera, and have you photograph the two turn points. If you were over them, you obviously got there. But in a big contest like this, they'll have ground crews at each point. They'll be spotting you with telescopes. And they'll have fluorescent signal panels, the kind air-sea rescue uses. They lay the panels out on the ground and every fifteen minutes, they change them around. When you get overhead, you make a note of the pattern you see below. That not only proves that you got there, in case the ground crew doesn't see you, but *when*."

Now they were on the flight line. Pilots were crawling into their tiny cockpits as ground crewmen sealed up the edges of their canopies with masking tape.

"The tape cuts down on parasitic drag," Barney said. "Every little bit helps. If you only pick up an extra half mile an hour that way, over eight hours that would be four miles. Many a soaring meet has been won with less."

Amanda helped Barney pull the Schweizer 2-32 out onto the runway. He handed her the extra parachute and began to slip into his own.

"Good thing I'm wearing slacks," she said, buckling the straps. "Did you ever have to use one of these things?"

"Not in a glider," he said. "Chances are I never will, because there's almost no place you can't get down safer in the sailplane than you can by parachute."

"Then why do you carry one along? I thought every pound was precious."

"So's my neck. The only time you'd need the chute is if

your ship broke up in the air. That doesn't happen often, but it does happen. Particularly in cloud flying. You see, Amanda, even though a glider is stressed, pound for pound, *stronger* than a Boeing 707, it's still possible to let your speed get so out of control in a cloud that you may not be able to pull out of a spiral dive without taking off your wings. That's when you wouldn't begrudge these extra twelve pounds one bit."

He helped her into the rear seat and made sure her harness was snug. Then he crawled into the front seat and adjusted his own belts. As a ground crewman approached, Barney checked all the controls. He moved the stick to one side and then the other to observe aileron travel; backward and forward to see the elevators respond. He kicked both rudder panels gently and nodded with satisfaction as he felt the panels move against the slight breeze.

"Hook up!" he called to the crewman, who attached a rope with a metal ring at one end to a claw-like device under the sailplane's nose. The crewman put pressure on the rope and yelled, "Pull!" Barney yanked a big red knob on the instrument panel and the claw sprang open, releasing the rope. "It's always nice to know the release is working," Barney said. "Otherwise the tow plane will have to circle you back over the field and release from his end. It's no fun trying to land a sailplane with a two hundred feet of nylon rope trailing behind. If it catches on a fence, it's goodbye Charlie."

Amanda laughed. "Is that part of your lecture on how safe soaring is?"

"It *is* safe," Barney said seriously. "It's just because we take all these precautions that we have fewer accidents per flying hour than any other form of piloting. Do you know the FAA lets a glider pilot solo at the age of fourteen? That's two years before most states will let a kid drive."

"I'm convinced," said Amanda, touching his shoulder. "Let's get this show on the road, before His Honor changes his mind and puts me to work."

The crewman had run down with the other end of the rope and hooked it to a waiting L-16.

Barney switched to transmit on his radio and said, "Bravo Foxtrot Tug, this is Bravo Foxtrot Air. Do you read me?"

His earphones crackled. "Bravo Foxtrot Air, I read you loud and clear."

"Ready for takeoff," said Barney Fields. He gave his shoulder straps one last tug, turned his head to smile at Amanda Webster, and waited for the sailplane to begin to roll.

3

Now it comes, thought Jan Makula. The Polish pilot was crammed tightly into the cockpit of his Foka 14. As the takeoff run started, Makula made large corrections in his aileron and rudder controls until they began to bite into the air. The wallowing gait of the sailplane smoothed and almost became flight. Jan breathed deeply, twice, and noticed that both of his feet were trembling slightly against the rudder pedals. Be calm, Jan, he told himself. It is too soon to become tense. This is only a practice flight. You do not even try for best time. Learn the air, study the landmarks. Watch the other pilots, discover their weaknesses. There will be competition enough when the real thing begins.

Makula eased back on the stick and the sailplane almost leaped into the air. Easy! Do not go too high. Stay out of the tug's slipstream. That's it, move off a bit to the left and keep the Foka down near the ground until the tug is airborne. Stay in low tow. It would not be friendly to dump an American pilot into the trees the way you did Franz Kepka. Poor Kepka, how surprised he was.

It had been Jan Makula's second solo, and he was flying an early Foka 2. The first solo, made after less than eight hours of dual flight, had come as an amazingly easy and anticlimactic experience. So, later in the day, as he walked out to the Foka, self-confidence glittered all over him. Ah, the stupidity of the young. What was he, on that long-ago day in 1954? Sixteen?

"Try to stay up a longer time, Jan," said his instructor, Franz Kepka. "You touched down in twenty-six minutes before. Stay up for thirty minutes and we'll get a 'C' badge for that empty lapel on your flight jacket."

The "C" badge mark of proficiency originated in the first German days of sailplane flight, and before long the FAI had adopted them as symbols of a pilot's skill. The basic badges, the "A" for a thirty-second flight in a basic, primary glider, and the "B" for a one-minute flight that included two ninety-degree turns, were hardly ever seen any more. But, in the early days of gliding when primary gliders were rarely launched more than fifteen or twenty feet into the air, the "A" and "B" badges were honestly earned. Now, the "C" with its three silver gulls on a field of blue, plus the identifying letter of the pilot's nationality, was usually the first award a fledgling pilot earned. Only Germany, because she had originated the badge system, did not use an identifying letter. The United States was "N," "CF" was Canada, "F" was France, and naturally, "P" was Poland. To earn the "C" required a soaring flight of at least five minutes *above* the point of release, and so a flight of thirty minutes assumed such a feat, since without soaring, the pilot would have been on the ground much sooner. Such a flight must be observed by an official FAI observer, of course, but all members of the soaring fraternity were authorized observers, and Kepka's signature would be all Jan needed for the glorious little pin.

But there were no soaring "C"s in the sky over Warsaw for Jan Makula that day. Where his first solo had been so smooth and easy, the second turned rapidly into a nightmare. When he eased the stick back on his takeoff run, the Foka 2 surged into the air as if propelled by rubber bands, and before he could reverse its movement he was caught in the swirling propwash of the tow plane. The turbulence twisted the Foka to one side, and with horror, Jan Makula saw the long tapered wing reaching for the ground, where it would dig in and cartwheel the sailplane over and over. . . .

In a panic, he let the Foka balloon up above the turbulence, and then he was looking down at the top of the tow plane and he could see Franz Kepka staring back at him and waving downward with his arm. The tow plane was too far along the runway to stop, and the stress of the ballooning glider had pulled its tail up into the air. Jan shoved the stick forward, and as the nose of the Foka dropped, the tow plane managed to struggle into the air, just clearing the fence. But Jan was still too high, and as the tow rope stretched and snapped forward like a huge elastic band, the nose of his sailplane surged into the air again and he was even higher above the tow plane than before. He could hear its engine laboring, almost directly beneath him, and he knew that the Foka 2 was out of control. He could not remember what to do to get it down a safe altitude again. He realized he was pulling the tail of the tow plane up into the air, putting it into a dangerous stall position, and then Jan realized with sickening certainty that there was but one thing he could do and that he must do it now.

He reached for the red release knob and, at an altitude of only two hundred feet cut himself free from the desperately straining tow plane. Instantly, the rush of air outside the cockpit dropped off to a whisper, and he pushed the stick forward to keep the Foka from losing airspeed and falling off into a stall that, at this low altitude, would be deadly. Soon he saw that the airspeed was safe, and it was time to look for a landing spot. Jan Makula noted that the wind was blowing from his left. And nowhere ahead was there a safe area to land. So he must turn. Easy. Slowly. Keep the nose down. Not too steep, do not lose any more altitude than you have to. The Foka shuddered slightly. Put that nose down! That was the very edge of a stall! Keep enough speed in the turn, or she will whip over and that will be the end. Now, there is the edge of the runway, coming into view. Where is Kepka? Did I release too late and dump him down in the trees? No time to look now. I must land. Keep the nose down. But not too far. The field is a long way off. Can I make it? I am flying only two miles above the stall, is that my minimum sink? I cannot remember. Where did all those numbers go? Here comes the fence. I am high enough, I will get over. No, I'm too high. It's downwind, and I am floating! I will run out of runway. How can I get her down? Dive? No, that will just build up excess air speed. Put on the spoilers. The spoilers! Of course. That is how I should have come down from my high tow position. Pulling them on destroys the lift of the wings. I am near the ground. But the field is running out too fast. Touchdown. Forward pressure, keep her down. Put her on the wooden nose skid, that will stop us.

There was a shuddering wave of motion throughout the ship and then a thump as one wing hit the ground and . . . silence.

The boy sat there, straining against his harness. He did not notice the tow plane landing overhead, dropping the tow rope only yards from the Foka. Jan still sat there with his head down when Kepka ran up and banged the canopy with his fist.

"Well, my young genius, you have done the impossible! You managed to beat the tow plane down. That will cost you two more dual check rides to learn how to get out of high tow. And we begin right now!"

Today, of course, sliding easily into the cumulus-filled sky over Eielson Air Force Base, Jan Makula had no difficulty keeping the Foka 14 in perfect low tow. If only his legs would stop trembling!

4

Well, this day is a boomer, thought Chet Cameron as the tow plane in front or him began bouncing up and down in a thermal less than a hundred feet off the runway. Not much like "merrie olde England," I'll say that. How many winch launches have I endured, at three and six each, only to make a single circuit and land because I couldn't catch a thermal? Not much chance of that in these parts! Catch those cumulus! Literal mountains of them, and a freshening breeze so we'll have those lovely thermals breaking free of the ground all day.

The tow plane turned slowly in the sky ahead. He felt

as he always did on aerotow: that he was a boy with a long, long string, and fastened to the other end of it was a tiny plane, and he was swinging the plane around in some fantastic game of crack-the-whip.

The air was clear. All around him were the tiny wisps of forming clouds. Far down to the southwest, he could see the magnificent hump of Mount McKinley. There were storm clouds around the mountain's crest, blue-tinged with distant flashes of lightning.

We'll see a proper wave over that mountain, he thought. The Russian can't sleep for dreaming about busting Bikle's altitude record. He may get his shot. Not that I'd mind a try myself, but fifty thousand feet without pressure? That's hairy. Maybe I'll give it a shake anyhow, at least high enough to get my altitude diamond. Fat chance of ever getting it in England.

He adjusted his controls slightly, to keep the tow plane exactly in the center of his wind screen.

How many pilots have won those three diamonds up to now? No more than two hundred, that's for sure. That isn't very many, but oddly enough, the field's started to feel crowded so I shouldn't be at all surprised to see them add another set of tasks. Perhaps three little platinum chips for flying a sailplane around the world.

I remember when I first began. Then, stepping up from the basic "C" to the Silver "C" was hard enough. You had to make a five-hour duration flight, and in those crates we had just after the war, that was no laugh. The distance flight was thirty-two miles, and you had to gain more than three thousand feet over point of release.

Chet Cameron smiled. It *had* been hard, particularly in the confines of England, but in the summer of 1953, he had won all three silver awards in a single day over York.

The Gold "C" had been a different matter.

That altitude gain of 9,700 feet ran away from me until late '64, when I got lucky and shot up through a big nimbus with both barographs ticking away. Good thing, too, because the ink trace on one was broken by the turbulence, and if I hadn't had the second barograph, the good old Swiss Peravia, making its trace on waxed paper, I'd have blown the whole show. On the other hand, the distance flight of 186 miles which should have been dicey was so disgracefully easy I was almost ashamed to accept the blasted badge. Almost, but not quite. What did Phil Wills, probably the best pilot England's turned out, call that kind of flight? A "vulgar downwind dash?" Although I noticed that good old Philip didn't scorn such a vulgar downwind dash when he swept down from Odessa, Texas, in the 1960 U.S. Nationals for his diamond distance. He liked it so well, he went out the next day and did the same thing.

Chet turned and studied the relationship of the airstrip to the sun. Just in case the compass packs up. . . . I wonder If I'll ever get my own badge filled up with diamonds? Maybe I'll get the altitude here.

He studied the cloud-covered Mount McKinley.

I certainly ought to be able to gain five thousand meters in a wave off that big bastard of a mountain. What is that in feet? Something over sixteen thousand–16,400 feet, to be exact.

I've already got my diamond goal, so it'd be nice to fill the old badge up with the other two diamonds here–the altitude and the five-hundred-kilometer distance.

Whoops, look at that tug go up! He must be in the granddaddy of all thermals. I'll wave my wings, let him know I'm going to cut free. It ought to be just about . . . here!

Then there came the shuddering crash of air pounding against the wings as Chet Cameron pulled the red release knob and turned into the first big thermal of the day.

5

ABC photographer Ben Wade unsnapped his safety belt and leaned far out of the circling L-16 to point his 16mm Arriflex at the sailplane which was being towed two hundred feet behind.

"Careful," said the National Guard pilot. "I wouldn't want to lose you."

"Don't worry," said Ben. "I bear a charmed life. Jesus, look at that bastard back there. He can't even sit up in that thing. He's flying on his back. Leave it to the Russians to do everything the hard way."

"From what I heard in the hangar, that's supposed to be a real high-performance sailplane," commented the pilot.

"Why not?" said Ben, burping off a few feet of Ektachrome EF film of the KAI-24. "The Russian government paid for the whole schmear. The way I hear it, the guys from the States and most of the other free world countries, have to pay for their planes out of their own pockets. One guy even designed his own and built it in the garage. And here they are competing with the whole damned Russian aircraft industry. Does that sound right to you?"

"Personally," said the pilot, "putting the money aside, I think it's healthy. Here I've been studying the Russians and spending my whole military career getting ready to blast one out of the sky, and now all of a sudden I'm towing one up in a glider and as far as I can see, he's just a guy pretty much like you and me."

"Bull," said Ben Wade.

"My mistake," said the pilot. "I should have left *you* out."

"Hey," yelled the cameraman, "He's wagging his wings."

"That means he's going to release the tow rope. Get your camera out there, start shooting. You'll see the rope springing free. There, I felt it go. Did you get the shot?"

"Dead center," said Ben Wade. "Hey, can you get in a little closer so I can take some air-to-air stuff?"

"Okay," said the pilot. "But not too close. I wouldn't want to wrap this tow rope around him."

He eased the L-16 closer to the soaring KAI-24 and, through the reflex finder of his Arriflex, Ben Wade could see the intent face of Major Anton Suslov as he zoomed in with the ten-to-one lens. Suslov tilted the all-metal sailplane into a gentle curve, searching for the center of the thermal he had just felt thud against his wings.

"Wow!" said Ben Wade. "What a shot!"

6

Americans! thought Major Anton Suslov, glancing at the cameraman in the circling L-16. What an amazing people. In one breath, they scream about security precautions and squander billions to protect the Alaskan skies from unwanted Russian intruders, and in the next, they invite an officer of the Soviet Air Force to fly a glider right through the heart of their vaunted Distant Early Warning System. Incredible!

But then my own countrymen were not so bright, either, selling this magnificent land to the Americans for a paltry seven million dollars. Alexander Baranof must spin in his grave every time an airliner takes off from Kodiak for Seattle. The poor old fool thought he was putting something over on the Americans. But why not? The Americans themselves took some time to realize what a bargain they had really won. "Seward's Folly." What folly! Given another twenty years, this land, which can grow a crop in six weeks, will become a paradise. One can become used to long winters and ice and snow and darkness.

I, of all men, should know that. I have seen nothing darker than Moon Base One in the lunar night. And then there were those bad years at Port Arthur, as a subaltern who had to beg for every little nut and bolt for my sailplane. Those days are gone. Gary Powers obligingly took care of that with his U-2. What was it, after all, but a huge sailplane with a little jet engine? The audacity of those Americans! I think they are perhaps a little mad, but I must admit that I like them better than I should. That big one from Texas. Barney Fields. He is a man himself, not what some committee would wish him to be. Perhaps there is hope for us after all, because I know there are many good men on our side, and it is a comfort to discover that the other side has some good ones too.

He turned his head and looked at the white side of Mount McKinley.

Will the great wave come? Will it come in time?

It must! This will be the time I defeat Mr. Paul Bikle. My elastic suit is not truly a pressure suit, because we cannot afford the weight of the support equipment. But surely I can survive another few thousand feet with its aid. I am a younger man than Bikle was in 1961, and I have better equipment. If only the wave comes. If I believed in God, I would pray that the wave should come. Perhaps I will anyway. It could not hurt.

7

Lucille Bowers abandoned her post at the mayor's office and drove her little Fiat out to the airbase to watch the sailplanes take off.

My God, she thought, I'm chasing him. And for no reason. He looked right through me. It's Amanda he's after. Bill must be blind. Inviting Barney to live with them, and letting Amanda spend hours up there alone with him in a plane!

It's not fair. One man comes along out of a hundred that puts water in your joints, and before you can even swoon into his arms there's another woman standing between you. And a married woman at that.

Now she's up there with him in the Alaskan skies, on their way down over the flatlands to Nenana. Then home. How long would it take?

Lucille remembered Barney telling her the sailplane might average around forty miles an hour, and how surprised she had been. He had laughed at her.

"Oh, it'll fly a whole lot faster than forty," he had told her. "But what you do in cross-country flying is circle in a thermal to gain altitude, then as soon as you've used up the lift, you streak down along your course looking for some more green air. That's when she can scoot along sometimes at seventy miles an hour. And if I find a cloud street, I can keep going at that speed without circling at all."

"What's a cloud street?" she had asked.

"A whole line of cumulus will build up downwind with good solid lift under each one. You can just shoot down the row, actually gaining altitude, and that really brings up your speed average."

She stared up into the sky. Was that a cloud street there now? A row of fluffy white clouds down to the south looked just like the condition he had described. Maybe he would make good time and be back even sooner than he expected.

But, of course, Amanda would be with him.

Lucille got back in the Fiat and drove downtown to Fairbanks.

8

The controls of the Ka-20 felt comfortably loose in Wolf Lindner's hands without being sloppy. The ship was handling well, and he had crossed the first turn point with more than three thousand feet in altitude. Looking down, he saw that the task committee had been clever. The signal panels were surrounded with a portable canvas wall, so that no pilot could read them from the side. To see them, you had to pass honestly over the check point itself. Yet the panels were large enough so that a pilot would not have to waste precious altitude getting low enough to read their message. Wolf checked his watch. The elapsed time was good. And his next leg, to the southeast, did not look too difficult. The third leg, the final hundred kilometers bucking the wind, would be the hardest. But the triangle had been chosen well. Unless conditions deteriorated fantastically, most of the ships should make it back to base. With his practiced eye, Wolf had never been out of gliding distance of a safe landing area. Of course, later when the flights took them through the mountains, landings would be more hazardous.

But there should be no difficult retrieves on this first practice flight.

Wolf remembered the worst retrieve of his flying kite. It was at his first international championship, and he still remembered the great honor he had felt when he learned he had won a place on the team. The month was June of 1958, and the place was Leszno, Poland, near where this year's meet had originally been scheduled. On the morning of June 25, the task was announced as Free Distance. The skies showed promise of superb soaring. Wolf drew a circle on the map of Poland and saw—as did most of the other sixty-two pilots—that Diamond "C" distance was possible to the northeast, and to the southeast. Both directions gave possible flights of more than five hundred kilometers before reaching the Russian border. But in the central part of Poland, the 312 miles needed for diamond distance would not be possible without flying over the Russian border.

It was well after eleven in the morning when Wolf got into the air, towed by an alarmingly short rope and a sturdy green Polish plane. And, once he released, Wolf had an almost perfect flight. He had a heading of northeast, which gradually changed to the easterly direction, but he was sure, as he flew over a vast checkerboard of grain fields and rolling pastures broken by small forest clumps and placid rivers, that he would easily exceed the five hundred kilometer mark. The terrain below was like one great landing field, free of danger, and Wolf was able to strike out across country with a daring he had rarely felt. The afternoon was glorious, filled with vigorous thermals under lofty white cumulus, and then best-speed dashes across the cloudless voids to the next area of lift. By late afternoon, when convection began to weaken, Wolf's flight plot showed that he had covered more than 450 kilometers. He began the last glide of the day under a dying cumulus and prepared to stretch it past the precious five hundred kilometer circle which according to his map was just ahead.

But also ahead was a roadless swamp, surrounded by scrubby trees. He could not even see a path from the air. Landing there would mean certain trouble in derigging the sailplane and getting it to the trailer. But if he didn't press ahead, he would fall short of diamond distance. Wolf decided to take the risk. He was flying his own ship; had it been club property, he would not have chanced the dangerous landing. Flying with the knowledge that he was risking the year's salary he had tied up in one fragile wooden sailplane, he stretched his glide until he literally flew the plane into the black muck of the swamp.

Two peasants from a nearby field, who thought they had seen a "crash" came rushing over to remove the body from the wreckage. Their booted feet splashed mud and water against the tapered wings as Wolf crawled from the cockpit. Since he knew no Polish, Wolf had to rely on his "understand form." He pointed at the phrase that said, "Take me to a telephone." But the championship sponsors had not considered the possibility that pilots might land in the fields of farmers who could not read. Wolf tried to pronounce the unfamiliar words, but that only confused the farmers even more. Finally, by picking up an imaginary telephone and dialing, he got his message across. One peasant stayed behind to guard the sailplane, and Wolf and the other man sloshed off through the swamp toward God only knew where. Two hours later, they reached a crossroad and, at it, a small hut. Inside, Wolf saw at once that there was no telephone. But the uniformed man there waved his hand, indicating that the pilot was not to worry. He handed Wolf one set of climbing irons, helped him strap them on. The uniformed man put on another set himself. Then, still not believing what was happening, Wolf climbed up a telephone pole behind the uniformed man, and found a portable telephone wired across the two cables. The man spoke briefly into the instrument and then handed it to Wolf, who almost fell off the pole when he discovered he was speaking to his brother, who had remained back at the base at Leszno. Explaining his situation, Wolf put the uniformed man back on the line, who apparently spelled out their location to a Polish official at the other end. Once they had lost track of his plane, Wolf knew that his retrieve team would begin phoning base every few minutes for news.

Shortly after sunset, the retrieve team arrived with the trailer. By now, a small crowd had gathered and this delighted Wolf, because he knew getting the Ka-5 out of the swamp was going to require manpower. The small mob followed him into the swamp where, in darkness, the retrieve team derigged the ship. Piece by piece, it was carried out the long, treacherous path to the road. It was well after midnight when the team set off back toward Leszno, and breakfast time when they arrived.

With a cup of coffee in one hand and his barograph, still sealed, in the other, plus landing forms signed by the two witnesses who had seen him come down, Wolf hurried into the operations office and laid his course against the official maps.

There could be no doubt about the results. He had been forced to land three quarters of a mile short of the magic five-hundred-kilometer circle, and had missed his diamond distance. And that was the closest he had been able to come since.

But he was determined to reach it this time, in the green air of Alaska.

9

Bill Webster stood with his back to the operations building, sipping a Coke. The planes had been out four hours now, and by the excitement around the radio shack, he assumed some were about to return.

He regretted urging Amanda to go with Barney Fields. But it had seemed the only thing to do. The hesitant, quickly withdrawn glances between the two had not escaped him. He trusted Amanda. He couldn't lock her up in a tower. So, under the circumstances, after Barney's invitation, there was nothing else he could have done.

But he was still sorry he had.

A communications man leaned out the window of the radio shack.

"Mayor Webster? We've got a blip on the scope. It's coming in real low."

Webster looked up. "Is it Barney?"

"No, he doesn't have a transponder in the two-place ship. Mike, you got an ID on this one yet?" There was a pause. "It's sailplane R.D., sir, that's Renée Duval, the little French girl. According the the poop sheet she's flying an Edelweiss C-40."

Webster turned back to watch the runway. "Thanks," he said.

10

I know this is not a competition flight, thought Renée Duval, reclining in the nearly horizontal seat of the Edelweiss and watching the altimeter unwind. But if I am first, it will be an omen. There is at least a half mile to the field, but I have more than three hundred feet of altitude. I will make it on final glide. And I will have best time, too, unless someone has beaten me down. That will wipe the polite smiles from their faces. Men! They think they invented the world.

She adjusted the trim tabs. This is a good ship, but a little tail-heavy, I think. I need more weight up here in the cockpit. I would hate to go into a spin. It might not be possible to get the nose down again to recover. It is all that new gear in the back. *Merde!* One should never graft equipment onto a plane like extra wings. If we had known transponders would be required, we could have had them designed into the modifications we made in Paris. I do not like having all that new weight back there.

As she saw the end of the runway just ahead, she thought, this is at least a good beginning. And I did not fly my best today. There was too much of that lovely champagne with our bull of a Russian last night. Why do I play with him? I think he could be very dangerous, and it is foolish to flirt with danger merely for the temporary thrill. Now, the American, that Barney Fields, he would be a better choice. But he did not even look at me.

Yes, there is the touchdown point, within easy reach. God bless you, André, for introducing me to this beautiful ship. I think you only did it because it amused you to see me lying on my back with the control stick seeming to make love between my outstretched legs, but we have had the last laugh, my Edelweiss and I.

Over the fence, now, very carefully. Do not flare too high, fly her right onto the ground. A little more spoilers, that will do it. Touchdown, and roll right down toward that truck, the one with the cameraman on top. Remember to give him a big smile.

11

"How are you doing?" Barney Fields asked.

Amanda Webster waggled the control stick slightly from her rear seat position. "Straight and level," she said.

"Very nice. Keep her lined up with that big cloud over there at eleven o'clock. We ought to find some nice lift underneath."

Amanda flew the Schweizer toward the towering cumulus. "Aren't we wasting time, Barney?"

"It doesn't matter," he said. "Enjoy yourself. Today doesn't count for points."

"It's another world," Amanda said. "If it weren't for the radio, one could believe we're alone on another planet."

Barney had been listening to the mid-air chatter of the other pilots. He laughed, and switched off the set. "There you go," he said. "Now, what's your pick? Mars? Or maybe Venus?"

"You're crazy," said Amanda. A small thermal rocked the plane. She turned toward it, tried to center the lift. But in seconds she had passed through the thermal and the sailplane was in down air. "Oh, Barney! The red pellet's up! We're sinking."

"Watch yourself," he said, "or we'll find ourselves down in that field."

"Take over," she pleaded. "I don't know what I'm doing."

"You're doing fine," he said. "Watch your air speed. We're a little low for stall recovery."

"Please, Barney!"

"What's the matter? Don't you want to spend the afternoon in a field with me?"

She hesitated. "It's not that. But—"

"You've got an even chance. Get us over that ridge, and I'll fly us home."

"What if I can't?"

"We've got a couple of sandwiches on board. And they'll find us sooner or later."

"You can radio them."

"From another planet?"

Her hands trembled around the control stick. Barney, she tried to say, this is silly. Let's have no games. I'm not available.

But she remained silent, and tried to find another thermal. If we go down, we go down, she thought. It won't be my fault.

"Okay," Barney said, "better let me have it. We've got to commit to a landing. It's too dangerous to spiral any more."

She watched his shoulders tense slightly as he resumed control of the sailplane. Ahead, she saw a sloping green field, filled with brightly colored wildflowers.

As the sailplane's wheel touched down and they began their rollout, one thought repeated itself in her mind.

I didn't plan this, Bill. I didn't plan it.

12

Along the 67th Parallel, where the Chukchi Sea meets the Arctic Ocean, a small Russian trawler plowed through the roughening sea, and the captain tapped on his ancient barometer to be sure the needle was really dropping as fast as it seemed.

"Something is brewing," he muttered. "It may be only a low pressure area, it may be a real storm."

But, he told himself, real storms don't happen in July. And it was very nearly July. More probably, it was just a front moving through. Or getting ready to move. Who in God's name knew about the weather, anyway? All one could depend on was that one could depend on nothing.

And, almost a thousand miles away, a brief wind nibbled at the peaks of Mount McKinley. For perhaps thirty minutes, an invisible wave of air hung suspended downwind of the mountain, and a small bit of paper blown from some climber's camp circled in the rising torrent of air and tumbled upward, until it was out of sight in the blue twilight of that last day of June.

JULY 1: *Opening Day*

1

THE governor of Alaska shook Barney Fields by the hand and said, "What did you think of my speech?"

"Great. You and the mayor make a real team."

First Bill Webster, then the governor, had spoken briefly to the opening day crowd about the outstretched hand of friendship offered to the competitors by the great state of Alaska, and the photographers and reporters captured every minute of it.

Now Barney Fields and the governor were standing near Barney's Skylark, talking low enough not to be overheard by the crowds thronging up and down the airstrip.

"Bill's a good man. I understand you managed to crash his wife into a field yesterday."

Barney bit his lip. He would never forget the contemptuous look Ron Smith had given him when, his radio "malfunction" repaired, Barney had finally called for a retrieve and had reported into the operations room after landing.

"You can fly better than that, Barney," Smith had said.

"I was giving Mrs. Webster some flight time," Barney

answered. "I got careless and by then we were too low."

"This is a competition," said the gray-haired taskmaster. "I hope you'll remember that for the next few days."

"Yes sir," said Barney, his ears red. What made him mad was that Smith was absolutely right. It was stupid, going down in that field.

Stupid, he thought, remembering Amanda's softness pressed close against him, but I'd do it again.

The governor had said something. Barney snapped himself back to the present. "What was that, sir?"

"I said the pilots seem like good men. Even the Russian."

"They are," Barney said.

"I wish I could take up the sport. But there's no possible way, over in Juneau. Too many mountains, too much water. It's too bad we can't get the capital moved to Anchorage. That would be a better choice, actually, now that we aren't so dependent on sea transport."

"I've always wondered what the capital was doing over there on the side of the state," Barney said.

"Well, used to be that was about as far as you could get on a year-round basis, coming up from the South Forty-Eight. But now, with the Alaskan Highway and air transport, the other cities are actually more accessible, and far more logical choices for a state capital. The move may come, but I'm afraid it won't be in my term of office."

"What's the hang-up?"

"The old-line Alaskan families. They stand against change. In my book, they're just a little piece of Nob Hill that got shipped up from San Francisco without noticing the move."

"Be careful," Barney warned. "Some of those TV boys have got long-range microphones."

"It doesn't matter. Juneau knows how I feel. It's stagnating, and I've said so in public before. Because of the way the city's locked in by the sea on one side and the mountains on the other, there's no room for growth. Do you know our population is only around ten thousand? Anchorage is up to fifty thousand and going strong. Even Fairbanks has twice as many as Juneau, and the important thing is that those two cities are *growing*, while Juneau just sits there."

"Wasn't it named after some prospector?"

The governor nodded. "Joe Juneau. He found gold there in 1880. Juneau's prosperity was built on gold. The city never really knew anything else. But even dinosaurs must die sometime, and the biggest and last mine of all, the Alaska-Juneau, closed down in 1944. That's a long time to live on golden memories. Our state needs—demands!—new blood to grow, and the solid citizens of Juneau still regard anyone who hasn't lived there twenty years as a *cheechako*, a newcomer. Right now, the city lives off the government. The biggest payroll in town is state and federal employment. And any time it looks as if that payroll might move to Anchorage or Fairbanks, those old-timers raise a ruckus that you can hear all the way to Vancouver. Do you know, there's only sixty or seventy miles of roads in and out of Juneau, and most of them go nowhere? Which is fine with the good citizens. Damnit, without the desire to get out of that safe little hole they're in, how can they expect the rest of the state to keep on supporting a city that is really nothing more than an extension of the South Forty-Eight? Juneau's best suited for tourists, the lazy kind, who think a boat trip up the inland waterway and a visit to the Mendenhall Glacier, and a beer or two at the Red Dog Saloon is what Alaska's all about."

Barney Fields smiled. "Governor, you're a man of strong opinions. What's your opinion of the fuss about the North Slope?"

"My opinion is that everybody on both sides have managed to foul things up. The oil companies moved too fast with their pipeline proposal. And now the conservationists have their heels dug in permanently. Both were wrong. An effective compromise is the answer. The country needs oil, and the state needs the boost in economy." The governor studied Barney. "Do you think you'll be able to help out?"

Barney wiped a speck of lint off the canopy of his sailplane. "I don't know what you mean."

"Don't you? Mr. Fields, you surely don't think I'm ignorant of what goes on in my own state."

Barney did not answer. The governor touched his arm. "Don't worry. It's private with me. You undoubtedly have reasons for your secrecy. The matter is closed, as far as I'm concerned."

"Thank you," said Barney. "I'm not up to anything underhanded. It's just that . . . certain parties might misunderstand."

"Say no more," said the governor of Alaska.

2

"This demon of the altitude record has possessed you, Anton," said Renée Duval as she sat with the Russian pilot in the shade of a hangar, waiting for the 11:00 A.M. briefing. "Why is it so important?"

Suslov shrugged. "I think I can do it. At any rate, I must try."

"Is it only because you want to beat the Americans? That would be so easy. You could place two sealed barographs in a decompression chamber and, over a period of hours, vary the air pressure within to simulate a flight to any altitude you chose. The FAI would be forced to accept the proof."

The Russian laughed. "Ah, you remind me once more that with all of our nationalistic differences, the world is still divided into two races. Men, who are what they are, good or bad. And women, who are the same everywhere. Does the end truly justify the means, pretty one? How many of you have explained your lack of integrity by the little lie that 'does no one harm'?"

She stroked his black moustache. "My good major, I hardly think even you have known all women."

"I have known enough," he said. "Do not confuse this realistic attitude of mine with antagonism. I am old enough to shrug and accept things as they are. I toast you, my dear. All of you."

Renée laughed. "You're playing with me. The liberated American women have a name for men like you."

His smile widened. "I would not advise you to use it, Renée."

"Seriously," she said, looking away, "why is it so important for you to beat this Paul Bikle? Perhaps he was merely lucky. Perhaps such a flight could never happen again."

"Bikle's luck was in being prepared to snatch success when it appeared. And my need to beat him does not stem from any nationalistic rivalry. It is my personal shame that I, a pilot with the resources of a great nation at my fingertips, cannot best a California man who works to buy his own sailplane, and who pursues the sport at great personal expense. I must try, if only to find peace in my own soul."

She traced little circles on his knee with her fingertip. "Your soul seemed peaceful enough last night."

"The soul of love and the soul of achievement are not the

same. Last night, the soul of achievement was asleep."

"Well, thank the soul of love for being awake." She paused. "Were you surprised when I came to your room?"

"Not in the least."

She stiffened. "I see. You took me for granted, then?"

"Not that, either. At the party, I watched a beautiful little butterfly, flitting from one flower to the next. I was pleased that she came finally to me. But a butterfly should always be careful, for some plants have poisoned thorns."

"Are you threatening me, major?"

"Never. I accept you as you are. But I should be careful with that tall American, Barney Fields. I know that women such as you are outside his experience. Perhaps he would be easily conquered by your magic. But the fun of the game is that one never knows. It might be you who would be conquered."

The French girl pulled back. "It would be easy to hate you," she whispered.

"Easier to love," he said, touching her for the first time. She softened, and they sat closer for a while, until the loudspeakers announced the morning briefing.

3

Amanda Webster sat near her husband at the edge of the runway, watching Barney Fields escort the governor through the parked sailplanes.

"I'm sorry," she said, for the third time that morning.

Bill Webster lit his pipe, cupping his big hands against the wind. "Nothing to be sorry about. Things happen."

She hesitated. "Barney moved out this morning. He'll be staying here at the BOQ."

Webster smiled. "Does that make a difference?"

"Bill, nothing happened."

"Not true. Oh, Amanda, I don't say he laid you, right there in the middle of the field. But don't tell me nothing happened. All I have to do is look at your face."

She was silent for a moment. "What are you going to do?"

"Do? Me? Nothing."

She whirled on him. "Why not? Don't you care?"

"Of course I care, darling. I care very much. But what do you want me to do? Lock you up in the cellar? Fit you for a chastity belt? You're a grown woman . . . a lovely, desirable, strong-minded woman, and I'm hoping this—fancy—will pass, and things will be like they were before."

"Why don't you go over and punch Barney in the nose?"

"For what? He's only half to blame, isn't he?" She did not answer. "Isn't he?"

Slowly, she said, "Yes." Then, "Going back to the way things were before isn't the answer."

"I'm sorry," he said. "I had no idea you were unhappy."

"I wasn't, Bill! It's just . . . oh, damn, we agreed never to make comparisons."

"Make them. What you're saying is that it was better between you and Harry. Well, I've asked myself the same thing. Was it better when Sarah was alive? I don't know. It was different. But I'm different now. We're both different. Older, more experienced . . . less inclined to take risks. Can we ever go back to what we were before?"

"I don't know," she said. "Let's talk about something else, Bill. What's this plan you've got for moving Discovery Day up to coincide with the end of the Championships?"

"It seems like a nice finish to the whole affair," Bill Webster said. "I know Fairbanks was actually settled on July 28th, but these days, what with holidays being moved around to make long weekends, I think we're justified."

Amanda laughed. "Maybe we are," she said. "But, dear, you've got your facts twisted."

"In what way?"

"Discovery Day commemorates the day the Klondiker, Felix Pedro, made the gold discovery that touched off the great gold rush."

Webster groaned. "My God, you're right. And here I've been telling the reporters the other story."

"You know," she said thoughtfully, "switching the date isn't such a bad idea. All that whoopee with the old-time costumes, and all you men wearing beards, will make nice material for the television people. Oh, but . . ." she added.

"What?"

"What are you going to do about the glider pilots? They can't be expected to let their beards grow and wear oxygen masks at the same time. What'll happen to them on Discovery Day?"

"The same thing that happens to any other *cheechako* without chin hair. I guess we'll just have to lock them up in the hoosegow."

4

"What's tomorrow's weather look like?" Captain Tim Sanders asked.

The weather officer, Colonel Harvey Jenkins, said, "Just about what we figured. We'll look for thermal activity beginning at around 0800 hours and, unless the Japanese current changes its mind and moves in, convection ought to continue until just around midnight."

Sanders whistled. "That means almost sixteen hours of good flying conditions."

"That's the way it looks now. Those pilots better be able to get by on six hours sleep. And watch their liquid intake. What the hell do they *do* in those birds? They don't have relief tubes, do they?"

Sanders grinned. "My information is they carry an empty plastic bottle. Listen, I've got to start setting up flight plans for my boys. What do you figure for the winds?"

"Locally they'll be out of the northeast. Not strong. Maybe ten, twelve knots. Do you think they'll put up that three-hundred-mile triangle for a task?"

"That's what Smith is figuring on, if the wind stays where it is. They'll keep the upwind leg, where we'll have most of the sailplanes going down, over an area with the highest concentration of airstrips."

"That sounds reasonable," said Jenkins. "It's a little different than figuring fuel consumption, isn't it? Well, let's get together at 0700 hours tomorrow to reconfirm everything."

"Right. Listen, Harv, if you're through with your witchcraft, what say we head on over to the officer's club and have an early lunch?"

"Good idea," said Jenkins. "But you forgot the briefing. I've got to wait until that's over."

"Okay. See you afterwards, at the bar."

"Pour one for me," said Colonel Harvey Jenkins.

5

"Where's Bill?" asked Barney Fields, helping Amanda Webster into his rented car.

"Downtown. He's got a committee meeting to move Discovery Day up to the eighth to end the Championships with a bang."

"Oh. I thought. . . ." Barney stopped.

"What?"

"Nothing."

"If you're wondering was he upset about yesterday, the answer is yes. And if he's going to do anything about it, the answer is no."

"Why not? If I were Bill–"

"But you aren't, my dear. You're wild and unpredictable. Everything Bill Webster is not. Bill goes by the book. In the air, in his job . . . even in bed."

"Listen, Amanda," he began, "I didn't mean–"

"No, we might as well get it said. If I were in Bill's place, I would have come over here and knocked you flat, or been knocked flat myself. But Mr. Webster has read all the nice books about how a woman is an equal and independent person, and if she wants to go her own way after seven years of marriage, why Mr. Webster can only stand back and wish her luck, because that is the *fair* thing to do!" She clenched her fist and struck Barney full in the face. "So there! Consider yourself knocked flat!"

He caught her hands. "Amanda!"

"Let's get out of here, Barney. I need a drink."

He started the car and drove toward the main gate. "I'm sorry, Amanda. I thought you wanted it to happen."

"Oh, poor Barney. Of course I wanted it to happen. Don't you see, that's why I'm so mad! Have a little pity, flyboy. Here I sit in the tattered shreds of my virtue and all you can be is *logical*!"

He tried to make her smile. "Mighty fine tattering, too."

"Don't patronize me. You sound like my first husband. He was a mean bastard, too."

"Look, honey, why don't we talk about the weather, or—"

"Don't worry, Barney. I won't get all weepy on you. It's been long enough that I can even talk about it. Harry was one of those dashing Air Force jet jockeys. The ground crew called him Steve Canyon. What *I* called him, you can imagine. Especially when he was gone for weeks at a time and came back from Tokyo or someplace else halfway around the world with that smug, satisfied expression on his face. But, Barney, don't you see? As mad as I got, it didn't matter in the long run, because it was *me* he always came back to. He was *my* man, by God, and I feel sorry for these new women who think being free and equal is the same thing. I loved possessing him, and having him possess me."

Gently, Barney said, "What happened?"

"He was up in Seward on some silly inspection trip. For God's sake, checking mess halls at the radar sites or something equally stupid. He lived through the earthquake, but then the *tsunami* came sweeping along the Kenai Peninsula at a hundred miles an hour, wiping out everything in its path. Cars, boats, freight trains, even houses, everything was washed inland. I should have been with him, but at the last minute I decided to stay in Anchorage and go shopping. I've never forgiven myself for that."

"Don't be silly," Barney said harshly. "What good would it have done for you to die too?"

She looked at him. "What good did it do for me to stay alive?"

"I think you can answer that yourself when you crawl out of all that self-pity."

Amanda laughed softly. "You're a mean one, all right."

"Why did you stay in Alaska? Why didn't you go home?"

"I guess because I'm mean, too. I felt like one man up in Seward. The TV reporters interviewed him just after the whole mess was over. When one reporter said it looked as if the town would never come back, the old man glared right at him and said, 'Mister, that bay out there, and the mountain pass behind us ain't named Resurrection for nothing.' It's corny, I know, but I couldn't just give up and let our lives here mean nothing. I met Bill, and I think I've been useful, more useful than I would have been stuck in the middle of a Los Angeles freeway on my way to the supermarket."

She kissed his cheek. "End of confession. And the lady feels much better for having made it. Thank you, Barney."

"Happy to be of service, ma'am," he said, waving at the air policeman as he drove out the main gate.

"Now, turn about," she said. "What exactly are you doing up here, Barney?"

"Looking around," he said. "I'm kind of in between."

"No Mrs. Fields back in Houston? Tell the truth."

"Not even an ex," he said. "I hope a few beautiful ladies left behind shed an occasional tear, but we never got near a justice of the peace."

"Why not?"

"Not ready, I guess. It seemed like I had so much to do, there just wasn't time to split my life up. There was my work, and the flying, and not enough hours in the day."

"You don't seem to have to work now."

"Like I said, I'm sort of in between. I had a pretty good job down there. I put a little nest egg aside to finance this trip."

"And the only thing you're doing up here is trying to win this soaring meet?"

Evading the question, he answered, "The most important thing right now to me is to beat the world's distance record."

Accepting his answer, Amanda said, "Well, you be careful up there, do you hear me? I know how safe soaring is and all that, but I also know that there's a big difference between flying for amusement and flying in competition. Don't push too hard, because as sure as Boeing made gremlins, some piece of equipment will go on the fritz, or the nutty Alaskan weather will do an about-face and it'll blizzard in July for the first time in history."

"Don't worry," he said. "Mrs. Fields's little boy was born a coward and I've been developing the trait ever since. What I want most to do is knock out the distance record set by Alvin Parker, 646 miles. There's another record that isn't in the books yet, around eight hundred miles, set by a couple of Russians flying formation. But if I beat Al Parker, I'll be happy. All I need to do it is a Free Distance Day with the wind in the right quarter."

"Which is?"

"Out of the northeast at the beginning of the day, and shifting into the north sometime in the afternoon."

"Where would you fly?"

"Southwest, to Scotch Cap."

"Scotch Cap!" she cried. "Why, that's down on the very end of the Alaska Peninsula. It's the doorway to the Aleutians. That's a thousand miles from here."

"About nine hundred and eighty-five," he corrected. "It won't be easy. I'll need everything on my side, even with sixteen or seventeen hours of flying time. I'd have to pick up a little wave over the Alaska Range and gain ground speed. From Iliamna Lake on down, I'd stay upwind of the Aleutian Range, ridge soaring when I could, and then with luck I'd pick up offshore winds as I went down the edge of the Peninspula. If I can average fifty miles an hour, I'd make it."

"It sounds pretty iffy all the way," Amanda said.

"Chances are maybe one in a hundred to make the goal. But if I only have to beat Al Parker, I can land around Port Heiden, and I figure my chances that way are around one in ten."

"You're crazy."

"All the way."

He stopped at a red light. She moved closer to him. "Barney?"

"What?"

"Bill's downtown. Why don't we go home?"

He hesitated. "I thought you were hungry."

Her fingers bit into his arm. "I am, darling."

6

"I think it is the nerves I hate most," Jan Makula told Chet Cameron. "I am not afraid of the air or of anything in it. It is myself I fear. That I might make the wrong decision, that I might panic. Then I begin to tremble, and I must win to calm the nerves."

"Balls," said the Englishman. "There's not one of us who doesn't get a bit finicky in the stomach at the start of a big day. Personally, I always take three or four deep breaths and it seems to work. Not that I wouldn't prefer *your* cure. Winning, that is."

Puzzled, the Polish pilot said, "But one must fly to win. What other reason is there?"

"Why, scads, old boy. Why not fly because you can drift along under a cloud at five thousand feet and open the ventilator and breathe air no other human has touched? My old chum, Phil Wills, wrote a book about soaring that he called *Where No Birds Fly.* He came at the title, don't you see, because birds never fly in clouds. But we do. Even more important to me is the fact that I can fly in standing waves. I can fly in dry thermals above an abandoned airstrip. Now, that's not just where no *birds* fly, that's where no *men* fly. Except for soaring types, that is."

"And that is why you soar?"

"Where else but in soaring can you find the satisfaction of scraping your way out of a miserable three hundred feet of altitude above a valley full of bloody boulders that could total your plane? Don't you feel great chewing your way slowly up to cloud base and setting off across country again, thumbing your nose at the silly power pilots and their smelly engines, shoving them along like a vulture with a propeller up its arse? Confidentially, chum, I don't really care about scoring during this competition, except of course I want to do the best I can for the team, you know. If it weren't for the team, I'd be just as content cruising along looking for a wave to take me up and win that blasted altitude diamond."

Makula shook his head. "You and Major Suslov. He has, what do you say, the obsession? The *need* to achieve that immense altitude."

"Not me, pal. I want my five thousand meters plus a little piece more in case there's barograph error, and I'll snatch up my bloody diamond and scoot off for home as happy as a clam."

Makula lit a cigarette. "For me, it is more complicated. My team and I, we are trained to win. It is of great importance. It is a matter of honor for my country."

"Balls," said Chet Cameron. "I love my country just as much as you love yours, but it's no national honor to win nor a bloody national disgrace to lose. That's not what it's all about."

"Not for you, perhaps."

"It shouldn't be for you, either. No wonder they call you chaps the Foka Squadron. Flying formation because you like it is one thing, but turning the whole sport of gliding into a military operation is a bit much."

"I am sorry to offend you, my friend."

"It's not *me* you offend, don't you see that? It's *yourself* you're giving the dirty end." Chet stood up. "Oh, hell, let's drop it. It's almost time for the briefing."

7

I do not like this business of a woman competing, thought Wolf Lindner. It is impossible for us to have the same friendly rivalry. We must handle her with feathers, or she can spoil everything. Leave it to the French, to fly in the face of tradition, and send this girl into the business of men.

Come now, Wolf, said another part of him. Be fair. What of the Englishwoman, Anne Burns? She flew to many records, and they excited no jealousy in you. What of the time she gained 29,918 feet at Kimberley, South Africa? You sent her a letter of congratulation, did you not? And while you are examining your soul, Wolf Lindner, consider the American, Betsy Woodward, who reached an altitude of 39,993 feet above sea level in that old-fashioned Pratt-Read sailplane. No, my friend, I think it may be that you have personal reasons to resent the French girl.

She does not take her flying seriously, he argued. She concentrates on the photographers and on the men around her.

She also came in first on the practice triangle. And an Edelweiss is not exactly a kiddie car. The girl knows how to fly.

Admitted. But she also knows how to do other things.

Aha, and you are jealous that she chooses to do them with the Russian instead of you. Poor Wolf. Without a woman for only ten days, and already you have become a dirty old man.

Enough of this nonsense. If she flutters those eyelashes at me again, I will haul her on my knee and give her a good paddling.

So what? She will probably enjoy it. Meanwhile, if your legs have not been destroyed by the beer, perhaps you would be good enough to move along to the briefing. One never knows. You might learn something.

8

The briefing was half over. Captain Tim Sanders stood before the assembled pilots. "It's been a tough design problem," he was saying, "and we're sorry we didn't have them here for the practice flights, but anyway, we're ready now to issue you your survival kits."

"Survival kits?" asked Chet Cameron. "What on earth for?"

"We think every contingency has been accounted for," said the Air Force officer. "But there's still the slight chance that one of you might go down in an isolated area and get lost from both our search planes and the radar boys. This little kit might be the difference between life and death by the time we find you."

"More gear," grumbled a Canadian pilot. "How much does the damned thing weigh?"

"Sixteen pounds," said the retrieve officer. A groan went up from the hangar floor.

"It'll fit directly behind your seat," said Sanders. "It was designed to mount on the transponder unit."

An Australian pilot asked, "What exactly do we have in this CARE package?"

"I've got one laid out here on the table," Sanders said. "Come up and look at it after the briefing. Most of the gear is cold weather-oriented. If you go down on the flat or in the tundra, you won't be in nearly as much trouble as if you crash on a snowcap somewhere. First, there's the outer wrapper itself. It's made of heat-resistant plastic, so you can actually light a fire under it and melt down snow for water. See this little pouch? If you haven't any firewood, we include some cans of tinned heat, you slip one into the pouch and melt away."

"Why can't we just eat snow?" a Danish pilot asked.

"You could. But you'd still need water for the rations. They're freeze-dried, and much lighter than ordinary stores. But to make them edible, you have to add water." He indicated the pile of equipment on the table. "You've got enough chow here to go you about ten days. Then we've included the usual kind of emergency gear, all as light as we could manage. Knife, saw blade, flares, compass. You can't depend on that last too much, I'm afraid. The deviation is murder this far north." He held up a pole. "Now, this is made of aluminum. It's collapsible. Run it up as far as you can and let this blaze orange flag wave in the breeze. Makes for better visibility, and what's more, it's a radar target. Our boys ought to be able to home in on you with no trouble at all."

"Why all of this duplication?" asked Renée Duval. "We already have radios and transponders."

"Well, Miss Duval, we're assuming the worst, that they're all on the blink." Sanders picked up one of the unopened kits. "Finally, if you're unlucky enough to go down in the water, don't open the kit. Just pull this red cord and a CO^2 bottle will go off inside and inflate the kit into an emergency life preserver. But the water is so cold around here that you'd die of exposure within five to ten minutes, so my advice is stay out of the drink."

"Gad, but you're cheerful," said Chet Cameron.

"That's it on the emergency kit," said Sanders. "I'll turn you over to the task committee now."

Ron Smith stood up. "The way things look, we'll be able to go for that 306-mile triangle tomorrow. We're planning on it, but there's a backup task just in case. You'll know for sure at check-in in the morning."

He looked around at his audience. "I'm sure you all know how unusual it is for both standard and open-class sailplanes to be equipped with two-way radios. Let me make it very clear that those radios are for use only to assist retrieves and in case of emergency. And by emergency, I mean just that. If you've lost all lift and are going down into a field, it's all right to call out your position so the retrieve plane can get to you faster. But if we monitor any team member using the horn to tip off his mates about better thermal conditions, the entire team will be penalized points. And don't think you can get around it by using your blasted codes, either. I don't want to hear any chatter at all. Except for dire emergency, all transmission between sailplanes is forbidden. What's more, ground transmissions to sailplanes are likewise forbidden. This is going to be one competition where the individual skills of each pilot come into play, not a game to see which ground team has the best meteorologist. You'll get the latest information we can provide just before takeoff. From there on, barring any sudden danger condition that might arise, you're going to have to judge your own weather. Now, I know this may seem hard. Especially for those of you who have come to rely on your teammates for help in locating thermals and lift conditions. I think such assistance is apart from the purpose of soaring, which is to cast one man and one plane into the same sky inhabited by his competitors with the same chances for success or failure."

There was a subdued murmur from the Polish team. Smith went on. "Of course, if you have trouble, it's a different ball game. That's when you'll have more friends around you than in any soaring meet in history. The Air Force will be sitting up there at fifty thousand feet, keeping track of your transponder signals. Your retrieve plane should never be further than half an hour from you. You have your two-way radios for final security. And, my friends, you have some of the best potential soaring conditions I've ever seen. If I'd known it was like this up here, I can tell you truly, I never would have wasted all those months back in the forties, waiting around El Mirage for a wave to build up. So good luck."

For a few moments, the pilots gathered around to collect their emergency kits, and then dispersed.

Captain Sanders came over to Ron Smith. "I've got a kit left over," he said.

"How come?"

"One of your pilots missed the briefing."

Smith ran over in his mind who he had seen in the audience. He drew a blank on one face.

"That boy's going to get himself in trouble," he said under his breath.

"Who's that, sir?" asked Sanders.

"Never mind," said Ron Smith. "Let me have the kit. I'll see that he gets it."

Later in the afternoon, he went out on the flight line and placed it on the front seat of Barney Fields's Skylark 12.

JULY 2: *Triangle*

1

"TODAY'S task," said Ron Smith, apparently speaking to all the pilots, but actually fixing his eyes on Barney Fields, "is a 306-mile triangle, out to Indian Village, down to Bearpaw, and home. It's your own decision whether or not to go over the downspur of the mountains just below Fairbanks. Going over them will save you some fifty straight-line miles, but you'll have to be able to clear about twenty-two hundred feet. From there on, you'll be over pretty good country. Stay south of the Tanana River all the way to Indian Village. If you're low when you get there, you'll find a good landing strip. Set down and call for retrieve. That's your upwind leg, because the wind has switched over to the northwest. But there's good landing all the way, unless you go over the mountains."

Barney looked down at his map. Why was Smith focusing on him this morning? He had found the survival kit in the Skylark but until now it had not occurred to him that its being placed there was any more than routine.

He and Amanda had gotten all the way to the house before he clapped his hand to his forehead and groaned. "Hell! I forgot about the briefing."

"Turn around," she said. "We'll go back."

He had looked at his watch and said, "No, it's too late. Besides, it's probably just the same old stuff. We get our task briefing tomorrow morning. One of the boys will bring me up to date."

Obviously, Smith had noticed his absence. But why was he making such a fuss over it? Briefings had been missed before.

"Once you make your first turn over Indian Village," Smith went on, "you'll be heading downwind. But you'll have some mountains to contend with. Here, this elevation is the highest you'll have to worry about. Almost thirty-two hundred feet. Halfway down to the second turn point, you ought to see this big body of water up in the mountains. That's Wien Lake. Use it as a check point. Make your turn at Bearpaw, using the Kantishna River as a marker, and head northeast. We'll have the cold beer waiting." He looked around. "Any questions?"

"Are the turn points marked?" asked Chet Cameron. "Or do we use our cameras?"

"Good point. Today, you can forget about your sealed cameras. We'll have ground crews at each turn point with the marking panels. On the other hand, if you believe there's any chance of your breaking off across country in search of some elusive distance award, by all means carry your cameras and be sure to turn them into the committee without breaking the seals. That'll be your way to prove any distance triangle you decide to set up on your own."

Barney Fields stood up. "Ron," he said, "I know it's only 0800 now, and that seems pretty early. But if you'll look outside, you'll see that convection is well under way, and has been for almost an hour. I wonder if we could take a vote on earlier starts? It burns my hide to see those juicy thermals going to waste up there."

"0800 is plenty early," said Smith. "Unless we call the Free Distance Day. We have one scheduled, and of course, if we should call one at the last minute, you can check in here any time after midnight and we'll let you know. Then you can take off any time you want. But it's your responsibility to organize your own ground crew and to alert Captain Sanders in sufficient time to prepare a retrieve ship."

"Thanks," said Barney, sitting down. What the hell's wrong with the old boy? he thought. He sounds like he's chewing nails.

Jan Makula got up. "Mr. Smith," he said, "Am I correct in thinking that once I have completed my triangle, I am to make a pass directly over the runway before going out for a second try at better time?"

"Correct, Mr. Makula. Except that rather than take a chance on our missing you, it's permissable for you to radio your intentions to your retrieve plane. That'll let him know what you're doing, and we'll pick it up on our command monitors. But," he warned, smiling, "don't let me hear you telling him how great conditions were over such and such a place. After all, you wouldn't want to tip off your teammates."

Makula smiled back. "Naturally not." He sat down.

"No more questions?" Smith's deep blue eyes scanned the room. The fliers squirmed in their chairs. "Okay, good luck. Pilots, man your planes."

2

Ben Wade sat at the end of the runway, his Arriflex BL mounted on a tripod and attached by a cable to the Nagra tape recorder. Ordinarily he would have had a sound man along, but that was more to satisfy the union than to operate the recorder in a static situation like this. Ben smiled. He knew where his sound man was at this moment. Shacked up with that blonde from the Polar Bear Bar down in Fairbanks. Ben would cover for him. It wasn't hard. The recorder started and stopped automatically in step with the camera. You didn't even need a slate boy to hit the clapboards together any more. A one-frame flash of light marked the film and a "beep" synchronized the mark with the tape. Quite a change from the old days, when going out in the field with sound meant a crew of four and a large trunk full of gear. Now one man could hack it, although Ben would need the sound man when he began doing interviews with the reporter who was arriving from LA tonight.

Ben's left shoulder ached. He wiggled it, and felt the crunching together of improperly-fitting bones. He probably had at least an ounce of shell fragments in there, too. A permanent souvenir of the Tet offensive in Vietnam. Ben's on-camera reporter had collected an Emmy for his coverage of the campaign, while Ben and the sound man settled for a raise in pay. And Ben didn't begrudge the reporter the honor one bit, because he'd been in every muddy hole and rice paddy that Ben and the sound man had crawled through. It just seemed a little unfair that it was always the guy out in front of the lens who got all the credit, as if the pictures had been taken and the sound recorded by some remote controlled machine.

He stared down the runway. Which one of those planes is the Russky's? Hard to tell from way down here. It wouldn't hurt my feelings any to see that stuck-up sonofabitch crack that beauty up. It'd be nice if I could be there to put it on film. Hell, how do we know that bastard hasn't got a whole wing full of cameras in that glider of his? Nobody inspected it, did they?

Here comes the first one. I know this plane. It belongs to that little French broad. Zoom in, get a closeup of her face as the planes lift off. There she is, right in the middle of the frame. By God, she sees me, too. Look at that smile. Good footage. That baby really goes for cameras. Maybe I'll ask her up to my room, invite her to examine my zoom lenses.

Here comes the next one. Great. It's the Russian. Should I give him a closeup? Hell no. What for? He's not worth the film. He's probably so weighted down with intelligence gear that he won't do anything worthwhile in this contest.

3

Major Anton Suslov saw the cameraman at the end of the runway and gave him a jaunty wave as he flew over. There seemed to be reporters and cameramen everywhere. Except in Renée's motel room, for which many thanks.

"You do not frighten me, Anton," she had told him as they lay naked, her head on his chest. "I have decided on the American. When you have killed yourself with your insane altitude attempt, he will be comforting and consoling."

"And what do you propose to do about the wife of the Fairbanks mayor?" he asked, reaching over the edge of the bed to take up another cold sip of vodka. "She and the American frolicked this afternoon in that convenient alpine field, or I am no judge of the softness in a well-loved woman's eyes."

"Leave her to me," said Renée. "I have experience with her sort."

"Doubtlessly," said Anton Suslov. "Well, please do not kill me off just yet. I have unfinished business in this world."

"Do you think I care for you?" said the French girl. "Poof! I enjoy you. You make my body tingle. In the saddle, you are a true Cossack. But care for you? I will dance on your grave."

"Take care not to fall in," he said. "It might be embarrassing to be embraced by a corpse."

"Stop such talk!" she said. "You are depressing me. Why are we suddenly talking of death? Where is the vodka?"

"You have had enough. Try a beer."

"Beer is for Germans."

"Also for fliers. Tomorrow will be a long day."

"And a dry one," she agreed. "I would take a bottle of cognac with me in the Edelweiss to fight the cold over the mountains, except I will probably find no room for it in the cockpit after all the *merde* the Americans have crammed into my poor little plane. And that last, the survival kid!"

"Kit," he corrected.

"Whatever it is, I think it will be the final straw. My poor little plane waddles like a fat old sow, she is so tail-heavy."

"Perhaps you had better move some of the gear forward," he said seriously. "A tail-heavy plane is not very safe."

"Oh, I will survive. Perhaps I will let the plane fly without me. There is certainly enough equipment there to take my place. Anton, give me some vodka or I will throw you out."

He sat up and poured her a small glass. "How did you begin with the sailplanes?"

"How does any woman ever begin anything? There was a man. He flew sailplanes, and I drove the retrieve car for him. Then I learned to fly a little, and soon there were many men who admired me, and I was able to give up the business of retrieving and let others retrieve for me. I was amazed to discover that I had a talent for flying. In my plane, in the air, I became the dominant one. It was my hand that turned the plane into the thermal or into the ground, whichever I chose. When the tail assembly of my ship gave way in the air, it was my choice to use the parachute or let the deadly ground reach up and catch me as I fell."

Suslov shook his head sadly. "You are not yet a woman," he said. "You are a little girl with the body and the sex of a woman, but you still believe it is fun to tease the boys and break their hearts, and you still dream of dying young because that is easier than waking in the night fearing the old age and darkness that will come to you as it does to everyone. If you understood life better, you would stop playing at it and start enjoying its riches."

"Oh, stop, Anton. You are boring me."

"And you bore me, my dear. Do you so underestimate me that you think you can set me against the American by your chatter? That in our battle with each other you can slide neatly by and snatch up the forgotten victory cup? Well, do not deceive yourself, my darling. I am too wise for you."

"Go home," she said, her eyes closed. "I am asleep."

He laughed, and got up to dress.

And now she was somewhere out there in the sky, following her tow plane like the tail of a kite. And he must catch up with her, and defeat her.

Suslov looked at his altimeter. It was holding steady at two thousand five hundred feet. Eielson Air Force Base was at 548 feet above sea level, and all competition tows were to be to two thousand feet above terrain, so he could release any time he chose.

Far in the distance, as they turned, he saw Mount McKinley, its frosty head poking through the clouds.

"Soon enough, old friend. Do not be impatient," whispered the Russian pilot.

4

By 0930, all sixty-eight of the sailplanes were in the air, and Eielson Air Force Base started getting back to normal. The airmen drifted back to their jobs at the accounting office, the supply depot, the motor pool, the aircraft maintenance hangars, the dozens of offices and miniature factories that are necessary to keep any installation running smoothly.

Today, forgoing the questionable delights of piloting a tow plane, Captain Tim Sanders was in the operations center, keeping track of his retrieve planes and the competing sailplanes with the help of a huge map of the state. Two airmen pushed little magnetic symbols around it.

"About half of the sailplanes are going the long way around the mountains," said one of the airmen. "One glider's down already, up in the foothills. We just got word that his retrieve is already under way, that he'll come back here and circle the runway before making another start."

"Thank you," said Sanders sitting down to a huge mug of steaming coffee. Over its brim he noticed a magnetic symbol on the map. "Who is that up there, near Birch Hill? He's off course, isn't he?"

The airman examined his chart. "That's Air Juliet Mike, sir. The Polish pilot, Jan Makula."

"What the hell is he doing?' Sanders asked. "Indian Village isn't that way."

"No sir," said the airman. "It sure ain't."

Sanders growled under his breath and sat back with his feet up on the crude wooden railing. This was going to be the first crisis of many. He could tell.

5 /

The Polish team had settled on a kind of extended formation, with the four ships strung out in a line, half a mile or so apart. Like the great soaring birds they were, none left his safe airspace until he was sure the one in the next quadrant had found equally safe lift. Their ground track was quite good in spite of their caution.

Usually, the four pilots would stay together for most of a given flight, then, according to plan, the Open Class ships would surge ahead to bring up their average time while the Standard Class planes played it safe and came in at their own pace.

Jan Makula led the team with his Foka 14. He ached to be able to use his radio. It was unfair of the task committee to forbid its use. Well, at least there was no rule to keep one plane from watching another's progress with the naked eye.

Today, however, Makula had altered the usual flight plan. At the briefing, with the winds in mind, he found himself thinking: the long way around may actually be the shortest. Except then you will have that much further to beat back into the wind. Perhaps there is another way. And, studying his charts, he found a possibility.

I will not go around the mountains, nor will I go over the barrier peaks. There is a third way. Due north, with the wind on my left. Past Chatanika, then turn west and down the valley of the Chatanika River. True, that is almost directly into the wind, but if my map is correct, there will be a series of ridges along the river canyon, and with any luck I will find slope lift and that will get me through the mountains swiftly and out over the many small lakes. When I make the first turn point, I will hope to be ahead in time, and then I shall continue according to the briefing.

As he turned away from the other sailplanes, which were scooting for the safe passage around the lower end of the mountains, Jan Makula thought, this may be a serious mistake. But if I am right, my score will be an extra bonus for the team. Of course, if I am wrong, I will lower their score tremendously.

He flew over the little community of Birch Hill, streaking between still-forming cumulus clouds at a best speed of nearly seventy miles an hour. Below, no one looked up, for the passage of his ship made not a sound in the violently blue sky. At the edge of the next cloud, down now to a thousand feet against the rising slope of the hills, Jan felt the solid thump of rising air against his wings. He watched the sensitive needle of his variometer. It indicated five hundred feet a minute up, and the green pellet in the other variometer was well up into its tube. Should I continue on into the cloud? No, the lift is not strong enough to waste the time. I will get enough height to be sure I can reach the next thermal and cut free. Speed, not height, is the important thing.

As he circled in the thermal, the wind drifted him back down over Birch Hill, and Jan Makula resented every foot of forward progress lost. He left the thermal as soon as possible and continued up the edge of the small valley, lowering the nose of his Foka to better penetrate the wind. The needle of the altimeter unwound, and he was becoming increasingly nervous when he picked up the nibble of another rising bubble of air. He turned into the thermal, centered it, and checked his variometer. Only four hundred feet a minute. That was no good. He would spend so much time gaining altitude that his overall time would suffer. Somehow, he had to make more speed.

His eyes squinted as he studied the contours of the land below. Ahead, another cloud was forming, and he could probably reach the rising chimney of air. For what? Another four hundred feet a minute? At that rate, he would do well to average thirty miles an hour. There had to be some other way. That ridge down there, with the wind on its far side. Might there be some lovely little bonus of a small standing wave waiting for him, just a few hundred yards on this side? Should he risk it? What if he was wrong? Could he then beat his way through the downdrafts on the lee of the ridge to get over into the slope lift on the other side? And if he failed, where could he land? There was a little clearing just beyond the stream. Yes, he could get in there all right. But would the retrieve L-16 be able to make it? Well, if not, perhaps they could use the snatch pickup technique. It was worth the risk. If he was to go down, better to do it now and perhaps get back to base early enough for another start, rather than to crawl around the triangle at the speed he was presently making.

The trembling in his legs intensified as Jan Makula lowered the nose of the Foka 14 and listened to the airspeed build up into a swishing kind of whine outside the tape-sealed canopy. The ridge across the valley was getting very close, and Jan began to doubt his decision. In another few seconds he would be too close to the ridge and too low to ever hope to get over it. Automatically, his mind began to go over the off-field landing check list.

Then, although his senses felt nothing, his instruments responded, and with relief, Jan saw that both variometers were in the green. He had flown into the hoped-for never-certain smoothness of a beautiful little wave. Sighing as the tension ebbed, he cautiously felt out the wave's boundaries as his altimeter circled upward and then, still using the wave lift, he turned his nose toward Chatanika and was still climbing at almost a thousand feet a minute as he sped along at sixty miles an hour.

6

Wolf Lindner probed the treacherous pass just east of Fairbanks. He let the Ka-20 slip within yards of the jutting rocks before he decided that he had not hope of getting through the pass. He turned the sailplane back into the valley, diving through the downdrafts in a search for more lift to get him back up into the sky high enough to penetrate those angry stones.

He wondered if the task committee would assign any actual mountain flying during this Championship. He hoped so. Of course, such tasks gave the advantage to those who were trained in such flying, but most European pilots, at least, were familiar with the close work required when your wing is only a few meters above the jagged rocks of the peaks.

This valley reminded Wolf of another valley, in Italy. Although he had not flown in the Engadine valley during the World Championships of 1948, his brother Kurt had. Wolf had been crewing for his brother. On the eighth day of the contests, thirty sailplanes sat on the starting line at Samaden, waiting for the phenomenom known as the Maloja Wind, which occurs when the moisture-laden air of the Northern Italian plain seems to take on a life of its own and is sucked up through the jagged "V" of the Maloja Pass and crammed into the upper Engadine valley like a scoop of ice cream into a cone. As it rises, the warm air condenses and, in the chilly heights of thirteen thousand feet above sea level, forms great heaps of fluffy cumulus clouds that spill out over the mountain peaks like cotton balls overflowing a basket.

Thirty ships took off that morning. Only twenty eight returned.

British pilot Donald Greig, losing height as he flew along the mountain wall down the valley over Chiavenna, decided to cross the valley to look for lift over where Mount Basseta drives a triangular wedge into the lowlands of the olive groves. Opposite the tiny village of Era, his variometer showed green air and, as Greig turned into it, one long, tapered wing seemed, impossibly, to snag against something in mid-air. A wooden tip flew off, and as the other wing surged upward, the plane went into a savage spiral dive and, unseen by any human eye, splintered against the stones on the slope below.

Donald Greig had flown into an unseen, nearly-invisible cable that stretched down from the mountain to the valley floor. It was used by the woodcutters to lower their logs to market. Greig did not have time to use his parachute.

On that same terrible afternoon, Kit Nicholson, another

British flier, soared close to the cruel peaks just below cloud base. Suddenly a fanciful gust of wind whipped opaque whiteness around him and he was flying blind. Perhaps he turned, perhaps he pulled back on the stick and tried to balloon out of the trap. All that is known is Kit Nicholson's ship stalled and fell flat onto the spine of Mount Bellinghera. With both legs broken and internal injuries, he called for help and was heard by passing shepherds who carried him down the mountainside to a tiny stone chapel. When his friends arrived, they were met by a doctor who lowered his eyes and said, "*Il est mort.*" He is dead.

Men die at any endeavor, Wolf told himself. Men have died before in sailplanes, and men will die again.

But, please, he thought, suddenly aware that he felt a nibbling, almost unheeded, premonition about this Championship, please not this time.

Still searching for altitude, he forced a smile. Leave it to the task committee to put up a triangle that fell only six miles short of diamond distance. Diamonds took 312 miles, and this triangle was only 306. Obviously, they were trying to keep this Championship from turning into a free-for-all for honors. That was correct, too. Let the Free Distance Days be the ones for the diamond-hunters. Yes, Wolf agreed, he would like to earn his own distance diamond. But not at the expense of failing to add up points for the team.

That valley floor is really getting too close to my wheel. There must be some lift somewhere. Look. There is a hawk. He sees me circling. He is flying over to join my super-hawk in my super-thermal. Poor misguided bird. I am sorry, my little feathered companion, there is nothing here but zero sink at best. Look at him sneer. He is thinking that the super-hawk is not so bright. But I have no pride. I shall follow him back to wherever he senses lift. Ah, watch the little fellow now. He is circling upwards, and as he reaches his thermal, so am I. We are not rising very fast, only three hundred feet a minute, but that is better than sitting in the weeds of the valley waiting for a retrieve.

Now I have nearly four thousand, and that should give me room to spare in that pass, even if the downdrafts on the lee side are still as strong as before. Yes, they are. I am sinking rapidly, but I will still have enough height to get through. Good. I will make it, if the wings are not too wide to pass through. That would be an embarrassment, to break off both wingtips.

It was close, but we are through, and now it is bright sunlight and lovely downhill country, all the way to the lakes.

7

"Do you have to fly so close?" complained Jake Huggins. The newspaperman's face was pressed against the rear window of an L-16. "I could have spit in her eye that time."

"Sorry," said the National Guard pilot. "I just wanted to be sure we had the right one. You *did* want to see how the French girl was doing, didn't you?"

"That's what I said. But couldn't you tell from say, ten or twenty yards away? That's what they paint numbers on wings for. That's why they put in those transponders. That's why you have a radio. What the hell am I doing up here anyway? All I said was that I'd like to see how the pilots were making out. Did you have to try to stuff me in Duval's rear cockpit? I could just as well be sitting on the ground talking with all of you on the radio. I must be crazy. I am an old man with a weak heart and weaker kidneys. Flying is for crazy young idiots like you who have nothing to live for anyway. As for me, I have an investment in Social Security. I've put so much in the pot, I'll be damned if I'll die before I make those bastards in Washington pay some of it back."

"I don't believe you, Jake," said the pilot. "I always read your column."

"That takes one worry off my mind," Jake said. "If you can read, then at least you ought to be able to follow the map well enough to get us home."

"You're not as chicken as you make out. I remember that story you did about the walrus hunt. You could have covered that one from the mother ship. You didn't have to go out in a kayak with one of the Eskimo hunters."

"That's all you know," said Jake. "Did you ever smell walrus blubber when they pile it up against the boiler? The Eskimo kayak was by far the lesser of two evils."

Banking the plane, the pilot said, "That's the turn point there, Indian Village. It looks like a couple of gliders are down on the airstrip."

"I wish *I* was down," Jake grumbled.

"Want me to land?"

"Hell no, you klootch-lapper! Let's fly this crate over to Bearpaw. Maybe there's some action there."

"Yes *sir*!"

8

Renée Duval left Wien Lake behind and headed down over the flatlands toward the second turn point. She had gained altitude in the mountains. She was at 4,500 feet, quite a bit higher than three stragglers who followed her.

The Edelweiss bounced slightly as she flew through a column of rising air. Should she go back for it? No, why bother. There was plenty up ahead. Touch the rudder pedals, just so . . . trim the ship forward. She still feels tail-heavy. *Merde!* There is no forward trim remaining. All right, she will just have to fly with a light nose. Those idiots with their electronics. None of it has been remotely necessary so far. I am forbidden to use the radio except for emergencies, and who on earth knows what that ridiculous transponder is doing back there. And as for their survival kit!

Where is the Skylark? Renée had been looking for Barney Fields all day. Has he gone down? Or is he ahead of me? Wherever he is, I know he is not like those pitiful fools down there behind me, tagging along, hoping for the scraps of my lift. If they do not find something soon, they will certainly go down. Good. The fewer who complete the task, the more points for those who do.

She had left Anton Suslov twenty miles behind, as he struggled back and forth on a low ridge, barely keeping his wings twenty feet above the rocks. Renée had plenty of altitude. She could have drifted over and, finding a thermal, circled in it to show him its location. But that would have been stupid. He would not have done the same for her. She smiled as she left him and pressed on toward Bearpaw. Now there were three more stray dogs, clawing along beneath, searching for her leavings. She hoped they would go down soon.

Thinking of Suslov, she wondered about Barney Fields again. She was determined to have at least one night with the American.

But what about the Webster woman?

Perhaps I should speak with her. When a woman is hurt, she will withdraw without explanation and be hard to find—

and harder to convince. And that would press loneliness on Barney, who could then be expected to start looking for other company. . . .

Yes, Renée decided. That might work.

But first, there was the little problem of the scavengers below. How eagerly they watch every turn of my wings, how passionately they echo my every circle. If this keeps up, they may yet grasp hold of my petticoats and pull themselves up here to safety.

Deliberately, she turned away from her flight path and headed for a field where, her pilot's instinct told her, lurked a column of descending air. When she arrived, her variometer proved her right, and precious altitude bled away. But the other three ships sped over to join her. From their low angle, they could not see whether she was rising or sinking. When they reached the area of sinking air, they found out, but then it was too late. One by one, they circled down into adjoining fields to wait for a retrieve. Two thousand feet overhead, Renée Duval broke away from her snare and headed for Bearpaw, leaving two New Zealanders and a German cursing under their breaths as they crawled out of their sailplanes onto the marshy mosquito-infested ground.

9

Chet Cameron found a cumulonimbus forming near Bearpaw. He had made his turn directly over the signal patterns, jotted them down on his knee-pad, and headed for home. If only I had another few thousand feet, I could simply lower my nose and make a beeline for the runway, sacrificing altitude for speed. What a boomer of a day! What time is it? Only oneish, and I've done more than two hundred miles already. Who ever imagined Alaska could be like this? Perhaps the weather is inclined to be freakish, but don't look the horse in the mouth, Chet old boy. They'll put up a Free Distance soon enough and then you'll cop that diamond. Or you might get it on the race to Barrow. Distance looks more certain now than the altitude diamond, although if our Russian major finds his wave, I'll be right there behind him.

Pay attention. Fasten your buttons on that nimbo there. It's still alive, no doubt of that. I'll wager she goes up to at least fourteen or fifteen thousand feet. What a pity we're on a time run, or I might get the altitude diamond right here. Still, I can use old fluffy to pick up another couple of thou to give me a straight shot at the airfield.

Chet crept up on the huge cloud like a hunter stalking a wary deer. As he drew closer to the swirling mists of the cloud base, he made a careful note of the sun's position so that he would be able to reestablish course quickly when he exited after a few minutes of blind flying. After all, one never knows what will happen to the compass or the gyros in one of those buggers. Ready. Instruments all set? Artificial horizon's on and steady. Electric turn and bank tickypoo. No oxygen, we won't go that high.

Well, let's get it over with.

Despite all the cloud flying he had done, Chet had never learned to enjoy it, and so he felt a tightening of his stomach as he let the Dart 27 swirl up into the blinding mists. Although he knew better, Chet still found it hard to completely disregard his senses and rely only on the instrumented evidence of his eyes. Now, as he tightened his spiral, his rear end told him that he was pulling out of a dive, but the instruments and his cold reasoning told him that he was circling in violent lift within the giant stem of the cumulonimbus. It was dark and wet in here, but he would not go high enough to hit the snow and hailstones he had visited so often before in English clouds.

Feel this bugger go, he marvelled. The Cosim variometer's green pellet is slammed all the way to the top of the tube. Twenty feet a second, maybe more, because the Memphis variometer with its clock face is reading somewhere in the neighborhood of two thousand feet a minute. I shouldn't be greedy, but at this rate of climb, I'll hang in for another minute or so. That'll give me altitude to burn on the downhill glide to the field. Seven thousand five hundred, eight thousand coming up. I'd better get out now. Level off. Center the horizon and ball-bank and fly straight out. My God, what turbulence! Sounds like the bloody wings are tearing off. And here comes the lightning. It's like sitting inside a kettledrum.

What's that other sound?

That's *slipstream!* Something badly wrong here. My horizon gyros must have tumbled because they read all whichaway. Look at that airspeed building up. Come on, don't panic. Try to get her flying level, or at least decrease the angle of the spiral dive. Do it now! Pull on those blasted dive brakes, you clown! Where has your head been? That's it, now the speed's coming under control. Of course, if the dive brakes hadn't done it, you could always have pulled her nose up and put her in a flat spin. If you can't get your speed down any other way, that's one way to get out of a cloud. But the brakes did the trick, he thought as the Dart fell from the side of the cloud into the cold air seven thousand feet above the Alaskan plains.

Chet put the sun above his left wing and after a quick estimate of his position versus altitude remaining, decided that he could reach the field while doing seventy-three miles an hour indicated air speed.

Smiling, he put the nose of the sailplane down and dove toward far-off Eielson Air Force Base.

10

Barney Fields decided against going into the thundercloud, preferring to cruise along under it with his eye fixed on another forming just a mile or so downwind.

Quite a few planes were down already, he knew. He had heard Anton Suslov calling out his position as he finally lost ridge lift and settled into a valley northwest of Wien Lake. Poor Suslov. He hadn't even made it around the second leg of the triangle. Well, tomorrow it might be Barney. On the chance that Suslov's retrieve plane hadn't read the transmission, Barney relayed it to communications center, who thanked him.

Yes, it's safe to head for the forming cumulus. Get your speed up across that empty area in between. There's probably sink there, so get through it as fast as possible.

Ah, made it. Feel that green air. Circle on up, go into the cloud a little. It's still forming. Where are we now? Sixty-three hundred feet. Is that enough to make a dash for the field?

Why not. Put the Skylark's nose down and let her go.

You ought to be on the ground by three. Take a break, then maybe you can take Amanda up for an hour or so. She's not a bad pilot. I could solo her tomorrow, if she does as well this afternoon as I think she will. I asked Pete Marsh to shoot wheel landings with her in one of the L-16's to get her out of the three-point routine. That's just about the only power habit we'll have to break her of.

Watch that airspeed, Barney old buddy! You're too anxious to get home. If you throw away all your altitude, you'll end up five miles short, and wouldn't *that* be a crock? Hold her right on sixty miles an hour. That ought to fly you right onto the end of the runway.

Who's that up ahead? It's a V-tail, pulling away. Damned if it's not that French girl in her Edelweiss. Now, I wonder if. . . .

Damn it, you've lost concentration again and your air speed is way to hell and gone again, and I wouldn't be surprised if you land short of the fence.

11

Renée Duval led the first day's competition with a full 1,000 points. Chet Cameron was second with 928, Wolf Lindner third with 914, and Jan Makula had an even 900. Barney barely squeaked in over the downwind fence and had 848.

The pilots headed for the showers, the beer at the officer's club, and the chow hall, in that order.

Renée posed for Ben Wade, who asked her to climb in and out of the Edelweiss twice, meanwhile manipulating the lever on his zoom lens and muttering, "Best damn crotch shots I've made in years." Then Renée vanished toward her motel, and the cameraman joined the pilots at the officer's club.

There had been casualties that day.

One Australian pilot gashed his forehead groundlooping

in a small field near Indian Village, but the ship was undamaged, and the backup pilot ferried it back to the airbase while first aid was being administered.

Ben Wade nearly became a fatal casualty. While following the Australian plane, shooting its forced landing, he leaned out and almost fell. The pilot yelled, "Drop the camera! Grab the strut!" Ben yelled back, still filming, "Like hell I will!" and if the pilot had not banked the L-16 swiftly, throwing Ben back into his seat, both Ben and his precious Arriflex would have fallen three thousand feet without a parachute.

A Spanish pilot stretched his glide too far and, lacking sufficient speed to get over it, landed in the middle of the air base's sewage disposal plant. Plane and pilot had to be hosed down several times before either were allowed to approach the retrieve team.

Of the sixty-eight planes that began the task, only twenty-one finished the full triangle and the conversation in the officer's club began to sound a little grumbly as the pilots lusted after the gold and diamond "C"s they knew were lurking in the green air around Fairbanks.

Shortly after 5:00 P.M., with the midsummer sun still high in the sky, Barney Fields and Amanda Webster wheeled out the Schweizer 2–32 and this time Barney let Amanda handle the full takeoff, only once having to shout, "Get her down! Get her down!" as she let the sailplane balloon too high on the tow. They released at two thousand feet and, without being instructed, Amanda located a thermal, centered it, and gained almost five thousand feet of altitude before breaking off and turning upwind toward the airfield.

"Hot damn, woman," said Barney. "If you'd been flying solo, that would have meant your 'C' badge. Oh, well. Why don't you see if you can put this baby into a spin?"

"No one can spin a sailplane," said Amanda. "I've been talking to some of the other pilots. It's impossible."

"Bull," said Barney Fields. "Stop showing the white feather and spin this bastard."

"Yes, fearless leader," said Amanda. She hauled the nose of the glider up sharply, pulling it into a sharp stall, and as the plane started to fall off on one wing, kicked in hard left rudder. The Schweizer flattened out and began to spin gently toward the Alaskan fields below.

"Good job," said Barney. "It's hard to put one in because of the relationship of tail surface to wing span. But one day you may *want* to spin one of these things. If you're caught in a bad scene and want to lose altitude without building up excess speed, this is the best way to do it."

"I hate to interrupt you, oh mighty teacher," said Amanda, "but that ground is getting mighty close."

"Well, don't complain to me about it," said Barney. "Get us out."

Amanda shoved in opposite rudder, waited until the spin diminished, then put the sailplane's nose down. Soon they were in an ordinary dive, and she drew the plane out of it with back stick pressure.

"Well done," said Barney. "Now, darling, unless you can catch a thermal, we are going to have to walk home."

12

Jake Huggins and Ben Wade were holding up one corner of the officer's club bar, shortly after midnight.

"Sure you don't want to stay up and watch the sunset?" asked Jake.

"Funny," said the cameraman. "What is it with you Alaskans? You're always laughing it up, taking it easy. Ain't you never heard of work? I hear you close down your goddamned newspaper when the salmon are running."

"I'll tell the world I do," said Jake. "It's a crime against nature to work when the salmon are running."

"You may not be so crazy at that," said Ben Wade. "Maybe I'll throw in the TV game and come up here and drive a truck. Then I'd have time to do some of the things I like, instead of what my producer lines up for me."

Jake looked at him in alarm. "My God," he said, "don't say that, not even in a joke. I hope you aren't figuring on going back to the South Forty-Eight and telling people to come up here to look for jobs."

"Why not?"

"Ben, if you send a batch of folks up here, they'll either starve to death or go on welfare."

"Who are you kidding? Everybody knows what a shortage of manpower there is in Alaska. We've all heard about the guys who came up here with nothing but a driver's license, put in a lot of that golden overtime, and went home with a bankroll big enough to choke a horse."

"I won't deny that never happened," said Jake. "But when it did, it was right in the middle of World War II, and maybe a little during the Korean war. But man, that was years ago. Those days are gone, probably forever. Those books and magazines you see with all the listings of high-paying Alaskan jobs? A big racket, my friend, and I'd put them out of business if I could. Do you know, back in 1959, a whole bunch of folks from Detroit, Michigan, all quit their jobs, sold their houses, and headed up here? They called themselves 'The Detroit '59ers,' and they must have thought they were the last of the big wagon trains west. Well, let me tell you, that was a pitiful sight. Most of them ended up on relief, and some of them who tried to put up their own log cabins had to be rescued by the Air Force when the flood waters trapped them."

"You old bastard," said Ben Wade, waving for another round of drinks, "are you going to sit there and claim that there ain't jobs to be had in Alaska?"

"No. I'm only saying there's no labor shortage up here. There are jobs to be had, but not for the unskilled laborer who's tired of swinging a pick in Seattle and thinks he might as well come up here and get paid five bucks an hour and enjoy all the hunting and fishing he wants. Once upon a time, when the government needed construction workers awful bad, some semi-skilled men had to be recruited from outside. But most of those guys stayed on, and any jobs that come up go to them. What I'm telling you, Ben, and I hope you pass it along, is that a man shouldn't come up here unless he has a firm job offer, and he should never bring his family until he's sure of a place to live. One family got up here and a week later, the police found them living in the back of their station wagon, taking turns at stretching out to sleep."

"Okay," said Ben Wade. "I get your point. Go ahead, keep all the salmon for yourself. Hey, what do you figure our glider boys will be doing tomorrow?"

"I'll find out," said Jake. He went to the telephone, dialed, spoke for a moment, and returned to the bar. "No telling," he said. "They're worried about weather. Whatever they do, it won't be a Free Distance Day."

"What the hell's a Free Distance Day?"

"A glider version of 'take your best hold.' The pilots can take off for anywhere they damned well please. The guy that gets the most miles wins the cigar. One of our pilots, Barney Fields, is all gassed up about that one. He thinks he can go pretty near a thousand miles, all the way down to Scotch Cap."

"Should I know where that is?"

"It's the last piece of God's green earth attached to the North American continent, that's where it is. Scotch Cap is the tip of the Alaskan Peninsula, just before you get into the Aleutian Islands."

"I'm impressed," said Ben Wade.

"What I want to know," said Jake, "is are we going to stay up and watch the sunset or not?"

"What time is it due?"

"Around 2:00 A.M."

"And what time does it come up again?"

"Couple of hours later."

The cameraman shook his head. "Doesn't hardly seem worth all the trouble, does it. Listen, old buddy, why don't we just have another drink instead?"

JULY 3: *Rain*

1

"SOME weatherman," said Ron Smith, staring out the window of the operations room at the drizzle that cloaked Eielson in a gray shroud.

Colonel Harvey Jenkins shrugged. "Can't win them all," he said. "If it's any comfort, the condition's only local, and it'll be pushed out by the circular air mass coming up from the southwest."

"Why don't you go out and tell that to my pilots?" asked Smith. "And take my advice. Go armed."

"I think I'll leave that up to you," said the Air Force officer, blandly.

Ron Smith leaned forward. "Colonel, this is important. Don't kid me. Are you sure we'll have a wind out of the southwest tomorrow morning?"

"Positive," said Jenkins.

"Okay," said Smith. "That lets me off the hook."

2

"Gentlemen . . . and lady . . ." said Ron Smith, "I'm sure, as you look out the hangar door at the Alaskan dew we're experiencing, your first impulse is to take your Jepson computers and stuff them down the throat of our eminent weather man." He smiled at Colonel Harvey Jenkins, who shrugged and looked embarrassed. "However, please restrain yourselves. The weather man giveth, and the weather man taketh away. He has chosen to give us liquid refreshment today. There's no point in even thinking of mounting a task. It's not scheduled to clear until later in the afternoon. So take the day off. And store up your energy. I promised you a task that would only be possible under the right conditions, and Colonel Jenkins assures me those conditions will be met tomorrow morning." With a flourish, Smith uncovered his task map. "So, to celebrate the Fourth of July, we've come up with a humdinger. By morning, the wind shift that started last night will be complete, and it will be coming almost directly out of the Pacific Ocean and the Gulf of Alaska. This wind condition will endure for at least thirty-six hours, and with this in mind, the task committee has put up the most difficult task of any soaring competition to date."

He traced it on the map. "A race of five hundred and two miles all the way to Barrow, Alaska, the northermost settlement in North America."

His grease pencil made a heavy black mark on the USAF Operational Navigation Chart. "This task will give you a little of every kind of flying there is. You'll have quite a bit of time in the mountains, and once you're clear of them, you'll have to fight for every precious scrap of lift there is, because there is damn little convection going on in the tundra country."

"Tundra?" asked Chet Cameron. "Isn't that kind of a swamp?"

"It would be," said Ron. "Except the permafrost—that's the underground mass that always stays frozen—is only a couple of feet under the surface. The topside gets kind of boggy, but it's solid down below. Don't worry, you won't sink in out of sight if you have to land. In fact, the big July thaw hasn't begun yet. That's no kidding, so if you have to go down, you won't have too much trouble finding a decent landing site. Just try to land as far away from water as possible, which won't be easy, because there are at least ten thousand lakes up there. The further from water, the more solid the ground."

He turned back to the chart.

"Now, after launch, you'll head west, just as you did on your Indian Village triangle. Once you get past that little spur of mountains, either by going over or around, you head up this pass, through the White Mountains, to Livengood. It's not much of a town, but you'll be able to spot it. Cross the Yukon River, which by the way will also take you across the Arctic Circle. Whoever does it first will set some kind of record, I believe, because I don't think it's ever been done before with a glider. Then turn west, above the main mass of the Ray Mountains, and follow this valley where the winter trail comes through. See it there? It's visible from the air. Then turn into the Endicott Mountains, head up past Gold Bench, up into this valley of the Tinayguk River, through the Anaktuvuk Pass, and breathe a hearty sigh of relief as you leave the mountains behind you. Now you'll be over the tundra, once you get past the Colville River and Knifeblade Ridge· It's only fourteen hundred feet, and shouldn't give you any trouble. Then cruise happily over a hundred miles or so of tundra, and you'll fetch right up at the point that leads to Barrow. You'll see Admiralty Bay to your right. There's a lovely strip up there, and while you're waiting for your retrieve, you might want to go over and see the monument erected to Wiley Post. He and Will Rogers were killed at Barrow, you know, when Post's plane, *The Wiley Mae*, lost power on takeoff. Any questions?"

A lean, tall pilot from Australia stood. "Just one. Like the kamikaze pilot said, 'Admiral, you out of your fuckin' mind?' " This brought a roar of laughter from the pilots. "I mean, sir, this is one hell of a challenge. It's diamond distance, and then some. I'm game, and I know the rest of the gang are. I guess what I'm asking is, do you think there's any real chance of any of us making the goal?"

"Mr. Hamilton," said Ron Smith, "I announced this as a *race*. Therefore, I, and the committee, expect at least five of the contestants to reach Barrow. Probably more. Conditions are perfect. You'll have a good deal of mountain flying at the outset, true. But no given portion of the task is beyond what you can reasonably be expected to handle. This is a difficult task, I won't deny that. But all I can say is I only wish I were in a ship myself."

"What best time do you anticipate?" asked Wolf Lindner.

"Twelve or thirteen hours, probably more. So we'll have flight lunches packed for you."

"More weight," groaned Renée.

"In closing," said Smith, "I can guarantee you that no

matter how long the flight takes, if you stay in the air, you'll arrive before sundown."

The pilots laughed and applauded him.

"What the hell's so funny?" asked Ben Wade.

"It'd be hard *not* to arrive before sundown," Jake Huggins told him. "This time of year, they've got twenty-four hours a day of sunlight up there. In Barrow, the sun won't set until sometime early in September."

3

"Barney, have you got a minute?" asked Bill Webster.

Just leaving the hangar, Barney stopped. "Sure," he said. "What's up?"

"I've been thinking about your offer," said Webster. "Of taking me up in that sailplane. Does it still hold?"

Puzzled, Barney said, "Sure."

"Good. Maybe when the weather clears up–"

Barney nodded out at the light rain. "This won't bother us. It's no good for cross-country, but it wouldn't keep us from doing some local flying. Want to give it a shot now?"

"The sooner the better," said Webster. "I guess it's time I found out what I've been missing."

Barney gave him a quick glance, but Webster did not seem to have any double meaning in mind.

"Let me arrange for a tow-plane," Barney said. "I'll meet you out on the flight line."

What the hell is all this about, he thought, going into the retrieve building. What's my friend, the mayor, up to?

He found Webster waiting near the all-metal, two-place Schweizer.

"She's a beauty," Webster said. "This is an American ship, isn't it?"

"Right. The Schweizer Company, down in Elmira, New York, makes it. They're the only major manufacturer of sailplanes in the country. They make the 2-22 also, a two-place, high-wing job that's been the workhorse around most soaring schools for the past ten years. It's a great plane, rugged as hell, which is what you need with a bunch of kids bouncing in from twenty feet up, and ground-looping every other day. It's not really a soaring ship. But this 2-32 is more than just a trainer, it's a true soaring bird with performance that equals some of the best single-place ships, including the little 1-26 that Schweizer's been selling for years. This baby takes soaring out of the solo class and makes it possible for the long-suffering wife to get up in a high-performance ship, even if she can't fly by herself. You have no idea how many gals have trailered sailplanes all over the world without ever getting a chance to ride in a really good one."

He opened the canopy. "Usually, I fly up front, but because I want you to see the instruments, I'll take the rumble seat this time.

"Now, get those parachute straps good and tight. Tighter. You ought to be bent over a little by their pressure." He helped Webster into the front seat. "Now, fasten your shoulder harness and lap belt. They'll keep you from getting tossed forward into the instrument panel or up against the canopy. Try to move. You can't? Good. You're supposed to feel like part of the plane. That'll help overcome your tendency to lean upward when the ship is in a bank."

"You make me feel just like I'm back in boot camp," said Webster.

"Good, because you are, Bill. One of the biggest troubles

we have with power pilots making the transition is that they feel because they can jockey a jet, a sailplane is small potatoes. It isn't. Now, see that red knob up there on the panel? That's to release the tow rope, and I'll let you do it, but keep the hell away from it during the tow. I know one idiot who thought he was opening the ventilator, and he released just as he was over the end of the runway. He landed on the top of a passing garbage truck, and it served him right."

Still talking, explaining, answering questions, the big Texan scrambled into the rear cockpit. The wingman lowered the plastic canopy and secured it.

"Open," called the wingman.

Barney said, "Pull the knob."

Webster did. "Close," said the wingman. Webster shoved the knob forward. The wingman gave a mighty tug at the rope. The sailplane jerked forward a few inches. "Open," called the wingman, still keeping tension on the rope. Webster pulled the red knob, and the rope sprang free.

"I feel just like we're in a sailboat, with one wing on the ground like this, heeling us over," said Webster.

"The wingman will get them level just before we go off," Barney said. "In an emergency, you can get off without a wingman, but it's kind of hard on the tips. Okay, here comes the tow plane. Now, rest your feet on the rudder pedals. Don't use too much pressure. I want you to feel what I'm doing. And just hold the stick with your fingertips. Good."

They were hooked up to the tow plane, and the L-16 crept forward until the rope was stretched out tautly.

"Okay," said Barney. "Notice how the wingman is waving the wing tip up and down? That lets the tow plane pilot know there's still rope slack to take up. Now he's holding us level. The slack's all gone. And here we go."

The 2-32 began to roll behind the straining L-16. The

single wheel hummed against the runway, and then the wingman was left behind and the sailplane was rolling along with both wings held level by the slowly moving air. In seconds, the sailplane was airborne.

"Now," Barney said, "here's where you'll find it's very different from powered flight. You notice that we're off the runway long before the tow plane. As soon as we get up to ten feet or so, we put in a little forward stick pressure to get back down. That takes some of the strain off the tow plane and helps him lift off. See?"

"A little forward stick my foot," said Webster. "It feels like you're diving us right into the ground."

"That's one of the hardest parts of the tow," said Barney. "Getting over that fear of the ground. We like to use low tow around here, so it's our job to stay down and let the tow plane climb up just high enough so his horizontal stabilizer cuts just above his engine mount. See? And stay off a little to his left. You have to be careful to stay out of the prop wash. Watch, I'll take her up a little. Feel that? It's the slipstream nibbling at our vertical rudder. So we just drop down a foot or so and we're right where we ought to be. Okay, he's turning. Watch the turns, don't over-control them or you'll slack the tow rope. Keep your nose pointed at his outer wing tip and you'll slide around real nice."

"What do you mean, *I'll* slide around real nice? I'm not flying this thing, Barney. You are."

"Sorry, Bill. You've been flying her since we got off the runway. Light on the controls, isn't she?"

"*You've* got the controls! I'm just following through."

"Well, don't let go of the stick to find out. Just turn your head."

Bill Webster looked over his shoulder and said, "Well, I'll be go to hell!" Barney Fields was leaning casually against his seat pack, both hands crossed behind his head.

"Keep it up, Mr. Mayor," said Barney. "You're doing just fine."

"Quiet," said Bill Webster. "Don't distract the pilot while he's trying to follow the tow plane without skidding all over the sky."

JULY 4: *Race to Barrow*

1

TWO hours after the day's launch, the World Championship Soaring Meet lost its first sailplane. It happened in the White Mountains, just north of Hess Creek, and by coincidence, Ben Wade was nearby to photograph the crackup.

An Australian pilot, Bob McBride, found his Boomerang FS-62 in desperate trouble almost without warning. He was soaring close to a rock-faced ridge, hoping to get past it and down into the valley of the Yukon River when a sudden wind gust tipped his fiberglass ship into a projecting rock, ripping away three feet of the left wing tip.

"Mayday!" McBride yelled into his microphone, twisting the crippled Boomerang away from the cliff face. "Romeo Bravo Air, mayday. Going down, one wing damaged. Mayday. Get a fix. One, two, three, four, five, four, three, two one. Romeo Bravo Air going down."

Ben Wade found the calm voice on the radio strangely out of keeping with the desperate words being broadcast. His press plane banked toward the mountains and, far below, he could see the crippled sailplane. He zoomed in, and the spinning white sailplane came into focus.

Another voice crackled in his earphones. "Romeo Bravo Air, this is Romeo Bravo Tug. Are you bailing out? Over."

"Negative," came McBride's calm voice. "Too low. I'm in a flat spin, and the airspeed isn't building up too much. I'll keep her turning until the last and then I'll try to stick a wing tip in the ground to soak up the impact."

The spinning sailplane filled Ben Wade's viewfinder. As the camera motor whirred, he saw one wing of the Boomerang drop suddenly and kick up a burst of dust from the rock-studded earth. The sailplane seemed to pivot on the wing, then hurled itself forward on its nose which crumpled back visibly. The ship settled onto the ground, looking like a broken cross.

"Romeo Bravo Air," pleaded the voice from the tug. "Do you read me? Over." A pause. "Bob, are you on the ground?"

"Romeo Bravo Tug," said Wade's pilot, "This is Press Plane Two. We're over the crash site. Going in for a landing. We'll keep you advised. Over."

"Press Plane Two, understood. We'll be there in around ten minutes. Good luck."

Fearfully, Ben Wade asked, "You're going to land down *there*?"

"Why not," said the pilot, nodding toward the crumpled sailplane. "*He* did."

The landing was rough, but the L-16 was still intact at the end of its bumpy roll. Ben and the pilot ran over to the crumpled Boomerang. It seemed impossible that any living thing could have survived the impact. But when they stripped back the shattered plastic canopy, a sunburned face looked up at them through already puffy, blackening eyes, and said, "If you took any pictures of this, mate, I'd appreciate a set for the Darwin Soaring Club. It'll be all they'll have to remember the old Boomerang by."

"Digger," said Ben, "you'll have them. In technicolor."

2

"Well, we lost one," said Bill Webster.

"I just heard," said Ron Smith. "Totaled. But the pilot got out with a couple of bent ribs. That's good luck."

"I knew it was possible," said Webster. "I guess I just didn't want to think about it. Maybe we made a mistake. Maybe this country's too rough for your kind of flying."

"Don't let it bother you," said Smith. "You're no more responsible than I am, or than each individual pilot. We know the risks, and we take our own chances. All in all, and no thanks to me, this Championship is better organized, better run, than any I've seen. For which we thank you and the governor. I wish I could say this would be our last accident, but no one can promise that. These are grown men and they know what they're doing. If anyone's to blame, it's me, for authorizing this race. It's unprecedented in soaring competitions, but in the judgment of the task committee, the conditions justify it. If blame falls on anybody's head, mine is big enough . . . and bald enough . . . to soak it up."

Webster poured two cups of coffee. "How did you get into soaring, Ron?"

"Well, after the war a bunch of us who had been fooling around with gliders got pretty serious about it. I guess it represented a rebellion against all those hours we put in flying C-47's and other heavyweights. I went into engineering, but it was really just to get money enough to build my own sailplanes. Guys like Steve Bennis opened air-fields and started gliding schools."

"Did you fly gliders during the war?"

Ron Smith grimaced. "Those clunkers? They weren't anything more than boxcars with wings. Remember all the newsreels of those poor bastards, some of them with only two and three hours of flight training, crashing those monsters into the hedgerows of Normandy? They set the future of soaring back twenty years."

He sipped his coffee. "Thanks. Well, I guess I really started even before the war, when I was just a kid, up at Harris Hill, in Elmira, New York, soloing in a Bowlus Baby Albatross. That's a funny little glider with a kind of pod for the pilot to sit in, and instead of a standard fuselage, it has a hollow boom running aft with the control cables inside. It looks sort of like a flying bathtub. There were damned few diamond badges around in those days. In fact, unless my memory is fouled up, they don't even exist until after the war."

"Barney seems very determined to get one of those diamonds."

"Well, the awards aren't valuable in themselves. What they do is measure your achievements. If you'll look at the SSA roster, the guys who were grabbing off the early badges read like a Who's Who of soaring. Bob Stanley got number one, the first American Gold 'C,' and his name heads the list on the plaque down in the Smithsonian. And there's Bill Briegleb, who designed and built his own ship, and even made it available in kit form for the rest of us. Wally Wiberg, Paul Bikle, Betsy Woodward. Steve Bennis, of course—he's got Gold 'C,' number 38, one number before Paul Schweizer, who's number 39. Paul and his brother, Ernie, set up the Schweizer Aircraft Company down in

Elmira. They build the best crop duster plane in the world . . . and, some say, blow all the profits turning out the only big-time American sailplanes. Without Paul and Ernie, the American soaring movement would have been in sad shape."

"Do many of you build your own planes?"

"Well, not too many actually design, although some of us assemble kits, particularly those from Schweizer. Briegleb designs, of course, and so does Dick Shreder. Dick would have been up here, if he hadn't hit that damned cable. But he'll be back next year with his HP-dash-whatever number he's working on this time. Without the Schweizer boys, that's what American soaring would be. A few supermen like Shreder and Briegleb building their HPs and their SISUs in the garage, which is fine for improving the breed, but a little rich for the average guy's blood. It's nice to have a major manufacturer in the picture."

"And you're still flying yourself?"

"You'd better believe it. I didn't make the U.S. team this time, though, and when Barney put out his call for help, everybody figured that I might be of some use in the task committee. More often than not, it's the task committee who have to take the rap when a meet goes off on the wrong track. We're feeling our way up here, I admit it, but I expect to see some real records set. And we'll have learned a lot about new methods of communications and retrieves."

"Don't jump on me for the way this sounds," said Webster. "I fly myself, as you know. But for me, it's always been a professional, no-nonsense business. That's why it seems kind of . . . well, childish . . . for a lot of grown men to be making such a fuss over a little gold 'C' or a diamond for it. It's not the same as if you were competing for a real *prize*."

"That depends on your definition of 'prize,' Bill. Most people, including Charles Lindbergh himself, say that he flew the Atlantic for the $25,000 prize that the London *Daily News* had put up. But the truth is that Lindbergh deliberately, and with the full knowledge and consent of his backers, took off from Roosevelt Field *before* he was qualified to receive the award. He deliberately forfeited the $25,000 prize and that was a lot of money in 1927—for another prize which was richer in his eyes. The prize of achievement, the prize of being first. That's what drives our Russian major crazy every time he looks up at Mount McKinley. The thought of taking Paul Bikle's altitude record away from him. Do you think I don't know that if that cold front decides to move in and we get a wave condition, Suslov will wave goodbye to his teammates and be off to the mountains in a flash? And Barney Fields can just *taste* that thousand-mile run he wants to make down along the Aleutian Range. So if you say, well, the diamonds are only little chips and what's more you have to pay for them yourself, you'll certainly be right. But you can't pay for, nor is there any way you can buy, the achievement that those diamonds stand for."

"I'm sorry, Ron," said Webster. "I guess I'm too used to counting things in dollars and cents."

"Stick to it," grinned Ron Smith. "Without them, we'd all be in a peck of trouble."

3

Major Anton Suslov could see the winter trail far below the wing of his KAI-24. The pass through the Ray Mountains was safely beneath him by almost three thousand feet, thanks to the lift he had found beneath a friendly cumulus and within its frothy interior. He was well above the Arctic Circle, and it gave him a pleasant feeling to know that he was one of the few glider pilots who could say he had flown in the Arctic.

Soon he would make his turn toward Gold Bench, the small village that would mark his portal into the Endicott Mountains and what appeared to be the most dangerous part of the flight, the attempt to beat his way over Anaktuyuk Pass.

Today, he was flying with his elastic suit tightly laced, although he did not plan to try for any altitude beyond that necessary to sustain the flight. But it was important that he become familiar with the suit so that when the real attempt was made, he would not be hampered by unfamiliar equipment.

Suslov had more than twelve hours of oxygen in the twin fiberglass tanks that were mounted behind his reclining seats. That would be more than enough for the job. As for the ship, she was as ready as she would ever be. And so was he.

Suslov sighed as he made a slight course correction. He had seen Renée sitting close to the American, Barney Fields, this morning at the briefing.

A thermal drummed against his left wing. Instinctively, he turned into it. Today, the prize would go to the pilot who could stay in the air. Leave speed to the fools. Milk every scrap of lift for every meter of altitude you can get. It is a very long way to that little tip of land projecting into the Arctic Ocean, and you will need all the help you can find to make that distant goal.

The bubble of warm air became unproductive at an indicated altitude of 7450 feet, and he turned on course again. The blue peaks of the Endicott Mountains were far ahead, beckoning him, inviting him into their rock-filled valleys and treacherous air currents.

As he drifted toward them, he heard the Australian Boomerang go down. Later, he heard the reports that the pilot was not seriously injured. Luck is still with us, he thought. But how much longer? Soon she may grow bored.

Let her do what she wants later, he pleaded. Just let me and my ship endure long enough for the wave to come.

4

This country is full of diamonds, thought Wolf Lindner. With any luck at all, I will earn one today.

The German pilot's Ka-20 was drifting down the gentle slopes of the plateau, toward the last elevation of Knifeblade Ridge which stood between him and the tundra. At least the mountain flying is over. The country ahead looks safe enough. But will there be lift?

With any luck, the flight was half over. Time for a sandwich.

He rummaged through his box lunch and found the usual apple. What I would like, he thought, is a cold bottle of Löwenbrau. But I will have to settle for lukewarm coffee from the thermos and a greasy chicken leg.

Let me see. This is the second task. If any of us make it to the goal, tomorrow will be a free day. Then another task on July 6. Under the new rules, that will make this a valid championship. And that will still leave July 7 for a fourth task, unless it is declared a rest day. Either way, we should be finished with the meet in plenty of time for the air show on the eighth, for the celebration they call "Discovery Day."

He felt a nibble of lift, and turned into it. A lovely little dry thermal with almost three hundred feet a minute in it. Which is not to be slighted, in these poor soaring conditions over the tundra. Watch it, part of your circle is coming out of the three hundred feet a minute lift into almost as much sink. Center up more carefully. There is no point in circling around here all afternoon merely to come out even. That's better, now the bad side of the circle is zero sink and you're getting almost four hundred feet a minute on the good side.

How long it has taken us to learn about the air in which we fly. It was only in the early thirties that the thermal became an important part of soaring. And it was not until after the War that the wave became a factor. I wonder what the next discovery will be. Even though we believe we have mapped all the oceans of the air, we can never be positive. Perhaps we will find some way to soar the jet stream, that invisible torrent of air plunging along five miles high and going at speeds of two and three hundred miles an hour. I am not convinced that the days of discovery are over.

Our little dry thermal is fading. I am not doing much better than holding my own. It's time to strike out cross country. I have almost six thousand feet over terrain. That will give me a distance of twenty miles or so before I am in trouble again.

Lower the nose. Do not hurry. Barrow will wait.

5

The four Foka sailplanes were strung out in a sloppy formation over the tundra. The group flying was working to perfection today. Now visual signals were used to invite other Polish pilots over to share the lift, or to warn them away if prospects were bad.

This is how the team should function, thought Jan Makula. As a precision unit, each part dependent and yet independent of the others. We will all bring home glory today. I am confident that I can reach the goal, and if I reach it, all will. See? Wroblewski has a good thermal, and he is signaling us over. We will join him, and before the lift dies, another of us will take on the exploration for new thermals.

There is less than eighty miles left to go. We will all make it.

6

My word, that's Admiralty Bay off there on the right, thought Chet Cameron. I must have picked up a few miles I didn't mark down on the chart. I'm ahead of my estimated time. There's less than thirty miles to go, and if I can only catch one more good thermal I'll be able to head into my final glide of the day.

My arse aches. How many hours has it been? Almost fourteen! The hours go by so strangely, when the day never ends. It's like flying on Mars. My watch says that it's almost 10:00 P.M., and it's like high noon up here. The sun won't set at all, they tell me. Of course, the poor blighters will get it on the other end, during the winter, when it'll be the land of always-night for a couple of months.

Do you think you might permit yourself a spot of gloating, Chet old boy? You've come far and away past the diamond distance.

This time we've got it, fair enough. Hell, we had it hours ago, if we'd wanted to set down in one of those mush lakes down below. If this is what the tundra looks like before the great goddamned July thaw, I wouldn't like to splash down there after the big melt.

Look at that blessed little green pellet. We've flown into a nice bit of lift, and if I can only work us up to forty five hundred indicated, we'll take off like a scalded duck for the goal. Forty-three coming up. Forty-three, five hundred. Forty-four. Don't poop out now, old girl. Only five hundred feet more.

Got it! Okay, get the nose down, and away we go!

7

Barrow, Alaska, is the largest Eskimo settlement in the world. Fiction meets fact there, where the natives still live by hunting and fishing. There are no roads into Barrow. To get there, one goes by air, by sea, or by dog sled.

You will have to look far today, however, for an igloo. A few still stand, but they are either abandoned or for tourist photographs. The Eskimos live in modern frame buildings which are centered around the trading post, the heart of the town.

Before the sailplanes began arriving, the population of Barrow was around twelve hundred. Now it was twelve hundred and five, with Chet Cameron, Wolf Lindner, Renée Duval, Barney Fields, and one Hungarian pilot lounging in the midnight sunlight at the edge of the airstrip.

"You pilots will fly back on a commercial airline," a retrieve pilot told them. "Wein-Alaska Airlines has invited you to be their guests. You'll spend the night at the 'Top O' the World' Hotel, and they'll haul you back to Fairbanks in the morning. Meanwhile, we'll get your sailplanes back to Eielson during the night."

"What about tomorrow's task?" asked Chet Cameron.

"There won't be any. You busted five hundred miles, and that means a day off for everybody. Enjoy yourselves."

One by one, the retrieve planes took off with backup pilots manning the sailplanes.

"I don't envy those buggers," Chet said, walking across the steel matting that formed the runway. "They've been awake as long as we have, and they've got a good six hours of flying ahead, even at redline speed."

A huge truck fitted out with fat airplane tires to keep it from bogging down in the mud pulled up. "Hop in," said the driver. "I'll take you downtown. You don't want to miss the *nalukatuk*."

Renée said, "*Nalukatuk*?"

"It's a big Eskimo feast dance," the driver explained. "They're celebrating the first big whale catch this year. They got nineteen big bowheads, chopped them up, and filled their underground storage caves with meat and blubber. Now they're set for the year."

"I thought we'd decided the United States wouldn't take whales any more," said Barney.

The driver shrugged. "Nobody told the Eskimos," he said.

Barrow was about what Barney had expected. Tiny frame buildings and dark, curving metal Quonset huts that had been erected by the U.S. Navy during World War II. As the truck drew closer to town, the pilots heard the shouts and drumming of the celebration.

"It sounds like they're really tying one on," said Chet.

"Let us hope they saved one drink for us," said Wolf Lindner.

"Look!" cried Renée, pointing behind them.

Circling over the airstrip, four sailplanes made their landing approaches.

"It's the Foka Formation," said Chet. "The little buggers made it this time."

"I'll go back and pick them up," said the driver. "Meanwhile, you folks get settled, then come on down to the *nalukatuk*. It's not often we have people dropping in all the way from Fairbanks in planes that don't have motors."

A bath, even with a sponge out of a basin, did much to improve Barney's disposition. He was pulling on his rumpled flight suit when a knock came at the door of his hotel room. He opened it and Renée slipped in, smiling.

"Since we share the world's goal distance record," she said, "I thought it might be nice to share something else." She held up a flask of cognac and sloshed it back and forth.

"Where did you get that?" Barney asked.

"My poor little Edelweiss was already so tail-heavy that I thought another few ounces wouldn't matter. Don't you have glasses here?"

He did, and they toasted each other, then the governor of Alaska, and the manufacturers of the Edelweiss, and, with the last drops, the Russians who, until today, had held the goal distance record.

"Speaking of Russians," said Barney, "I wonder what happened to Suslov?"

"Poof. Who cares? Maybe he ran into his precious wave."

"Not today. The chances are that he's down in the tundra somewhere."

"In that case, they will pick him up. Lean back, my Texan, and let me massage your neck. You are very tense."

"It's a long day."

"And a longer night. Why are you tense? Here you are at the very crown of the world, drinking fine brandy, and you have a girl's arms around you. Like this."

"Mmmm," he said. "You smell good. How did you work that, after fourteen hours in a sailplane?"

"A woman's secret," she said.

"What say we go down and have a gander at the *nalukatuk*?"

"In a while."

"What else did you have in mind?"

"This," she said.

8

Twelve pilots made the goal, a triumph of their own skill and a tribute to the audacity of the task committee. There would be considerable and heated arguments at future sessions of the FAI as to how a world's distance goal record can be split up among twelve pilots.

Major Anton Suslov missed Barrow by forty-three miles, and was brought into town aboard the retrieve plane. He had a bath and then went down to the celebration looking for his fellow pilots. He found ten of them, but Barney Fields and Renée Duval were missing. Suslov raised one eyebrow, but said nothing.

"Put 'er there, pal," said Chet Cameron, mellow from a few glasses of Eskimo hooch. "I love everybody in the whole world today. Sorry you didn't make it all the way in, old man. Except, that would have made thirteen, of course. But anyway, you got your distance diamond. And by God, so did I! Isn't this a hell of a Championship?"

"Yes," said Suslov. "I have never seen such conditions."

"They may change, though," warned Chet. "One of the old Eskimos over there warned me that there's a change of weather coming. He says he can feel it in his bones. Maybe that cold front will come down out of the northwest, and you'll get your mountain wave after all."

"In that case," said Suslov, "I drink to your Eskimo friend."

And the old Eskimo's bones may have been right, because far up to the northwest, where the Arctic Ocean gives way to the perpetual white of the ice cap, a frontal system of cold air finally broke free of the jet streams that had been encircling it and, hesitantly, began to move.

JULY 5: *The Free Day*

1

"WHAT are those?" asked Renée. "Can those be icebergs?"

Barney and the French girl were standing near the dock at Barrow's windswept harbor. Although it was 4:00 A.M., the sun was bright and the Eskimo celebration was still in full swing.

"I hear the ice only breaks up for a couple of weeks during the middle of summer." Barney said. "That's the only time the ships can get through."

"How long does summer last?" she asked, slapping at an insect.

"Not very long. From killing frost to killing frost, the average is around seventeen days." Renée slapped at another insect. "Here, you'll never get any peace from those things swatting at them. Let's go over by the fire."

"What are they? They're biting me, but I can't see them."

"Those are the punkies. Some people call them the 'no-see-ums.' They're actually tiny flies. One time they invaded Valdez and the whole town had to close down. Even the ships stopped unloading."

"Ugh!" she said. "I can imagine why. All right, you win. Let's join the party."

They strolled up to the fire that was at the center of the Eskimo celebration.

"Ah, there you are," said Chet Cameron. "Out walking in the sunlight, eh? Well, draw up a whalebone and have a drink. Eskimo hooch, Barney. It'll grow hair on your vocal cords."

Anton Suslov stepped forward. His voice was quiet. "Good morning," he said, looking at Renée.

"Hey," said Barney. "You made it. Great."

"I did not fly all the way on my own, unfortunately," said the Russian. "But I am here all the same." He studied Renée intently.

"What's that you're drinking?" asked Barney.

"Some of Chet's hooch. He is acting as liquor warden for the rest of us. He claims he can speak Eskimo, and although we all know this is a lie, somehow he manages to make himself understood. In fact, his old Eskimo friend has promised me a change in the weather."

"And you'll get it, too," said Chet. "He's never missed yet. Of course, that might be because he always predicts that it's going to get colder, and sooner or later, it *does* get colder."

"I see you aren't drinking, Renée," said Suslov. "Not talking, either?"

"How are you, Anton?" she asked tonelessly.

"Very well, my dear. I do not like this hooch as well as vodka, but one cannot have everything, can one?"

"I wouldn't know," she said. "I usually get what I want."

"For the moment," he said. "After that, who knows?"

"Excuse me," she said. "I'm tired. I think I'll go back to the hotel."

"I'll walk you there," said Barney.

"No, you stay and have fun," she said. "I will see you

later. Perhaps you can help carry the major when he drinks himself into unconsciousness. These Russians are not to be trusted with liquor, I am told."

Suslov lifted his glass to her as she strode off in her blue flying suit, walking like a man with long, loose strides.

"I drink to your success," he called after her. "Both in the air and in bed."

"Hey, buddy," said Barney. "Don't you think you're being a little rough?"

"Forgive me," said the Russian. "It is to be expected that you would defend her. I commend you. You are a good man, and you do not deserve to be treated in this cavalier fashion. I apologize, my friend."

"Thanks," said Barney, "but I don't know what the hell you're talking about."

"One day you will," said Suslov, half dozing by the fire.

"He's as boiled as an owl," laughed Chet Cameron. "Prop him up so he doesn't fall into the fire and cook his bloody bod."

"He's all right," said Barney. "Well, how does it feel to have your distance diamond? I presume your barographs were operating all right, or you wouldn't be grinning from ear to ear."

"I checked them the moment I landed," said the Englishman. "They were ticking away right as rain. And if my old Eskimo friend is right and we get a shift in the weather, I might go for the altitude diamond in the major's wave and get the whole show sewn up all at once, thanks to you, old chum. I understand this was your idea, holding the Championships up here, and a good plan it was too. This flight proved that. What I mean to say is that a lot of blokes will owe their diamonds to Barney Fields, and I for one am happy to drink his very good health."

"I, too," said Jan Makula. "My team and I myself honor you, Mr. Fields. Your aggressiveness had made this great day possible for all of us. Is that the right word, aggressiveness?"

"I rather prefer foresightedness," said Chet. "Or perhaps, even vision."

"You guys are putting me on," Barney said, but he was pleased nonetheless.

"No, we're serious enough in spite of the hooch," said Chet, waving his glass. "We know damned well who we have to thank for this glorious green air of Alaska. My God in heaven, imagine setting a distance goal of five hundred and two miles, over the blinding mountains and the frigging tundra and all, and having twelve ships complete the course! That's fantastic, and it's all thanks to this unbelievable state of Alaska and to Mr. Barney Fields."

"If you keep this up my head'll get so big that I won't be able to get it in the cockpit," said Barney.

"Excellent," said Jan Makula. "That will mean less competition for the rest of us."

"I'll be a ring-tailed raccoon," said Chet. "The Squadron Leader has a sense of humor."

"Pardon?" said Jan.

"Drop it," laughed the Englishman. "I knew it was too good to last."

"Chet," said Barney thoughtfully, "do you think there's anything to that old Eskimo's idea about the weather?"

"Seriously? Well, old chum, I wouldn't be at all surprised. A lot of those ancient types, they've been around so long that they're like a ruddy walking barometer. The old mercury goes down a couple of points and they don't have to look. They can *feel* it, in their bones. And I mean that literally, what with all the old healed fractures they must carry around under that grizzled skin. Until the white man came, if they read the weather signs wrong they were dead. I don't know if there is a weather-detecting gene, but if there is, it'll be the one that has survived up here."

"You miserable limey," said Barney, "I ask you for a serious opinion, and you rave on about genes."

"Sorry, old boy. What I meant, actually, was that a lot of the weather instincts must stick down in the subconscious of these fellows. A shift of wind, a wisp of cloud, a little extra moisture in the air . . . it all feeds into the old primitive computer and, zing, out comes an answer: 'It'll be colder.'" He laughed and drank deeply.

"I don't know if I'm ahead or behind," said Barney, "but either way, I'm going to quit. I just hope if we do get a change, that the winds come out of the northeast. That's the direction I need."

"Northwest is what the good major's dreaming about over there," said Chet. "Listen to the blighter snore. You know, for a Russky, he's a good sort. After all the propaganda we've been fed, I wouldn't have been surprised to find he had two heads. I hope the poor bugger gets his wave. Hell, now that I got my diamond, I hope everybody gets everything they want. I'm generous tonight, I am."

"Which reminds me," said Barney. "Despite the sunlight and those screaming Eskimos, it's almost five in the morning. I think I'll sack in for a couple of hours so I'll be in shape to fly this afternoon."

"It's a free day, mate. No tasks to complete."

"No, but I've got a new student."

"Ah, yes," said Chet. "Our eminent mayor. Well, if I were you, *I* wouldn't turn my back on him. But that's your problem."

"What's that supposed to mean?"

Chet looked away. "Nothing, old man. Just shooting my ruddy mouth off, with no right. Drop it."

Barney got up. "Maybe I'd better wake up our Russian friend."

"Leave him be," said Chet. "He looks so happy there, dreaming about his altitude record. I don't have the heart to disturb him. I'll watch out for him, chum. And since it's highly unlikely I'll ever be in this part of the world again, I'm going to sit here and enjoy my hooch and watch the crazy Eskimos do their war dance. See you in the A.M., old man. The airplane's due at nine, and I'll pound on your door. If you're not in the proper room, then you're on your own, you lucky bugger."

"Chet, you have a dirty mind."

"That I do," said the Englishman. "And the missus is a mindreader. So I don't dare play around. But she can't stop me thinking about it. And to tell the truth, this is the first time in my life I've ever had the urge to prang a fellow pilot. You'll give me a blow-by-blow, I hope."

"My lips are sealed," Barney laughed, getting up.

But, walking back to the "Top O' the World" Hotel, he knew he would not have joked so about Amanda. Yes, Renée was beautiful and indeed she was passionate, but it just wasn't the same. He felt ashamed. Chet would have nothing tomorrow to delight his genial voyeur's mind, because Barney would not go to her room tonight.

He did not have to. She was waiting in his, stretched under the blanket with her short hair tousled on the single pillow. As he came in, she opened her eyes, and when she stretched both arms into the air the blanket fell away and he saw that she was ready for him.

2

"There's no doubt in my mind," said Colonel Harvey Jenkins, discussing the weather with Ron Smith and Captain Tim Sanders, "there's a front up there all right, and it's started to move. By morning, you can expect winds out of the north. They'll swing around later in the day. The front ought to come through sometime on the seventh, and that'll be the end of good soaring conditions for several days."

"The boys will chop off our heads if we don't give them at least one Free Distance Day," said Smith.

"Then it'll have to be tomorrow," said Jenkins.

"Sure as hell, someone'll go more than five hundred miles," said Smith. "So under the rules, the seventh will have to be a rest day. And by the eighth, you say everything will dry up?"

"I'm certain of it."

"Well, a free distance task will make this a valid Championship," said Smith. He smiled sadly. "I wish I were free to try for distance myself. With the wind coming out of the north, those guys can go almost anywhere. Most'll head over toward the Yukon Territory, I guess. We'll have one hell of a retrieve problem. Any reservations, Tim?"

"None," said Sanders. "If they can get into a field okay, my boys will get them out."

"Okay," said Ron Smith. "We're boxed in, so there's no point in screwing around. Let's get the weather information down on paper and post it as soon as possible. I'll announce the Free Distance Day so the pilots can start planning their flights. Everyone's back now, except for that batch who spent the night up at Barrow. When are they due, anyway?"

"The Wein-Alaska plane took off at 9:30," said Sanders. "They ought to touch down here in another half hour."

"From what I hear, they partied it up most of the night," said Smith. He smiled. "Well, why not? It isn't every day of the week that you break a world's record. The lucky bastards. I envy them."

"One thing worries me," said Sanders. "The backup pilot reported to me that Miss Duval's Edelweiss flies tail-heavy. And he weighs a good fifty pounds more than she does. That's a potentially dangerous condition, especially for spin recovery."

"I'll have her add some ballast in the nose," said Smith. "And she'll blow a fuse. But we can't have her tail-sliding all over the sky."

"Mr. Smith!" said Tim Sanders in mock anger. "Watch your mouth! I'll have you know you're speaking of the woman I love."

3

"Are you going flying with Barney again?" asked Amanda Webster.

"Probably," said her husband.

"I suppose you think that's clever."

"Amanda, I don't think anything. Barney was good enough to offer to check me out, and I accepted."

"Crap!" she said. "Who do you think you're kidding?"

"Amanda," he warned. "Don't press it. I'm trying to keep things from coming to a showdown. It's not easy. You have to help."

She softened. "Oh, Bill. You're right. It's all my fault. You ought to black both my eyes."

Blandly, he said, "Discovery Day plans are coming along. Did you notice this two-day fuzz along the edge of my chin? It isn't much, but it'll keep me from being heaved into the hoosegow. The only thing is, I'm afraid it's coming in white."

She stroked his jaw. "Nonsense," she said. "You might call it salt and pepper, but that's all. Besides, white in a man's hair is very distinguished."

"I don't want to be distinguished," he said. "Besides, this isn't my hair, it's my chin whiskers."

"You'll look marvelous. What are you going to tell the television people about the festivities?"

"Oh, the usual bunk. We'll have people panning for gold along the streets facing the Chena River. All the merchants will dress up in frontier costumes. I presume you'll be a dancing girl, the same as last year."

"Maybe painted woman would be more suitable," she said.

He ignored her. "And, naturally, we'll toss any male over twenty-one without a beard right into jail. Of course, we'll have to release the pilots after an hour or so, because in the afternoon they're going to fly over from Eielson and put on a show over Fairbanks International. Then they'll land, and we'll have the Championship award ceremonies. After that, back downtown, and more whooping-it-up in the streets. Free beer at the Malamute Saloon."

"Sounds like a busy day," Amanda said. "Will you be glad when it's all over?"

"I mean to tell the world I will," said Webster. "The publicity's been great, but when everything quiets down, I think I may go off in the bush for a couple of weeks and just drink beer and fish."

"That sounds wonderful," said Amanda.

"Will you go with me?"

Amanda looked away. "Bill . . . I don't know."

4

The plane from Barrow landed shortly before noon. Although the Wein-Alaska route ordinarily brought the airliner to Fairbanks International, the plane was given special clearance to come in at Eielson.

After shaking hands all around with Ron Smith and Bill Webster, the pilots scattered to check out their sailplanes. Skilled though the backup pilots might be, no one really trusts his ship with any other flier.

Barney found his Skylark 12 in pristine condition. In fact, it had been washed and the plastic canopy had been polished. Oddly, he felt a little jealous, as if strangers had been touching something extremely personal.

The Free Distance Day had already been announced, and the pilots were excited. The operations hangar was full of fliers, checking their personal maps against the larger, official one. With winds predicted out of the north and northwest, conditions were ripe for one of Philip Wills's famous "vulgar downwind dashes."

"Me for Watson Lake, over in the Yukon Territory," declared Chet Cameron. "It's over seven hundred miles, and what's more, I can speak the bloody language."

Several pilots opted for Whitehorse, also in the Yukon Territory, almost six hundred miles away. That was enough to break the record set on the previous day's flight to Barrow.

Few saw any real hope for success in the route Barney Fields chose, down along the edge of the Alaska Range, the length of the Alaska Peninsula, then along the upwind ridge of the Aleutian Range, until he ran out of land at Scotch Cap. The terrain there was rugged, he knew, but hopefully he could double back to the strip at Cape Sarichef after he had photographed his furthermost point of travel.

Barney did not meet Renée's eyes. None of this was lost on Major Anton Suslov, who did not seem to have any interest in plotting out a long-range course. Instead, Suslov studied the contour maps of the Mount McKinley area.

"Good show," said Chet Cameron. "What's the drill now, chum?"

"Well," said Barney, "why don't we go downtown for a real steak?" If he spent the afternoon with Chet, he would not be tempted to see Renée.

"Wouldn't mind that at all," said Chet. "I'll organize us a car so we won't make the bloody taxi drivers rich beyond their wildest dreams. What do you say we get together in half an hour at the Officer's Club, where I'll stand you one of your monstrous martinis, and then head off to Fairbanks and make a proper afternoon of it."

"Well," said Barney, remembering, "not too much of an afternoon. I've got a date to fly with the mayor at five o'clock this afternoon. It wouldn't do to show up blasted."

"Right you are," said the Englishman. "I'll pull back your hand if you reach for one too many. See you later."

Barney managed a casual nod at Renée as he left the hangar. She returned it, an arch expression on her face.

"Your American seems to be bailing out," said Suslov.

"He will be back," said Renée. "He likes the scenery."

"And how do you like it?"

"He is incredibly crude," she said. "But almost pure in his innocence. It is nothing that you would understand, Anton."

"You might be surprised at how much I understand," he

said. "I have known innocence too, my darling. I would say that the principal difference between us, you and I, is that while we have both left our own innocence far behind, I still have respect for it while you see it only as something to corrupt."

"Anton, you sound as if you disapprove of me."

"I think that I do, Renée. I am disturbed by your little game. It has gone far enough."

"Jealous, Anton?"

"No, not jealous. Disgusted might be the proper word. I think your private contempt for life is becoming real rather than pretense. I once told you that you were a little girl playing at life and death. Now I think you have become dangerous. You are the same little girl but now with a loaded pistol in her hand."

"So? What do you intend to do about it?"

"Perhaps I will take the pistol away from you, Renée. Or perhaps I will let you play with it until it kills you. I have not decided."

"My," she said, smiling tightly. "The big strong Cossack is jealous."

"I am angry," he said. "I am angry with myself for permitting you to play this game. End it, Renée. Do not make me fight you."

"I end nothing," she said. "And please do not try to threaten me. This is not your Bolshevik Russia. There is nothing you can do to me."

"Do not be too sure," he said. And something in his voice made the hackles on her neck rise. She turned away from him and pretended to be busy with the weather maps. After a while she heard his footsteps going away.

5

Wolf Lindner sat in the Officer's Club, sipping his second beer. It was cold against the roof of his mouth, and he savored every swallow.

Free Distance Day at last. Now I will have a chance to test my skill against this beautiful country on my own terms.

Wolf had not yet decided on his goal, but he knew that it would be downwind, and that meant either the Yukon Territory, or a dogleg, along the Alaskan Panhandle and down into British Columbia.

He sipped his beer, smiling.

It will be a flight to remember. Certainly someone will go beyond five hundred miles, and that will make the next day a free day. By then the front will have moved in and the Championship will be over.

Wolf reviewed his position in the meet. He now stood in sixth place, and the German team was in fifth. A series of good free-distance flights could bring them up to third, or even second, but he did not see how it could be possible for them to wind up in first. He himself could do no better than fourth, even if he won a full one thousand points for free distance, which was not likely.

I will wager on the American, Barney Fields, bringing in the day's best distance. The audacious flight down the peninsula has no right to succeed. But I think it will. My instincts are usually right. But, he thought glumly, not so right that I would dare to set off for Scotch Cap myself.

One thing still bothers me. That nibbling feeling that

things are going too well. The crash of the Boomerang was unfortunate, but at least no one was seriously injured. I do not think that is enough to satisfy the gods. There will be other tragedies.

Wolf ordered another beer and reapplied himself to his flight map.

Yes, the dogleg down into British Columbia looks more and more tempting.

6

Jan Makula sat in the Officer's Club with his three teammates and discussed strategy.

"I think we can reach Whitehorse with safety," he said. "So one of us should declare that as a goal. Then, if the other pilots are not lucky, we have a chance of bringing home the goal record. Now," he went on, indicating the map, "if you project the flight track on out into the Yukon Territory, you can see that Watson Lake sits just beyond the seven-hundred-mile circle. The Englishman, Chet Cameron, has announced he will declare that as his goal, but there is no reason why one of us cannot also claim it. All right, if we get that far, and have daylight to continue, it will have to be down into British Columbia, between the Cossair and the Rocky Mountains. To be honest, I do not think we declare any goal beyond Watson Lake. Past that, we simply go for distance and hope for the best."

The other pilots agreed with his tactics.

"Our formation flying worked splendidly yesterday," said one. "I presume we will continue to use it tomorrow."

"Agreed," said Makula. "I would only suggest that we increase the distance between planes. Our Fokas have sufficient penetration to get through down air fast enough to go from one thermal area to another without losing too much altitude. But flying as close together as we were yesterday, there's an increased danger of two ships going down in the same sink. I almost landed in the mountains yesterday because there wasn't room to maneuver out of the sink without crashing into my wingman."

"I was about to suggest the same thing," said another pilot.

"Finally," said Makula, "it will be wise to alter our flight path as conditions change. If necessary, even abandon the goal. After all, points will be awarded on the basis of total distance. Let Chet Cameron carry home the goal distance record if he is able. What is important to us is that our team should win the championship, and if that means losing the goal distance, then we should lose it."

The pilots nodded. "Any suggestions?" asked Jan Makula. "None? Then may I thank you for your fine flying until this moment, and in advance for the great effort you will put up tomorrow. I think it would be profitable to spend some time this afternoon polishing the ships to eliminate all the drag we can."

7

"I hope those cats back at ABC network aren't cutting up my negatives," said Ben Wade. "I think I've got enough footage to blow up to 35mm and turn this into a theatrical feature."

"What do you expect from those clods at ABC?" asked another cameraman. "Now, if you'd come to work for a good shop like NBC. . . ."

Jake Huggins, who was lunching with the cameramen, asked, "What's the reaction down on the mainland to the Championships?"

"Pretty good," said the NBC man. "Everybody's rooting for a favorite pilot. Believe it or not, Major Suslov has a fan club in Beverly Hills. Of course, the deep coverage we're giving it helps. The film clips have been moved up from the sports slot to the regular news portion of our shows."

"ABC too," grunted Ben Wade. "I just hope they ain't cutting up the original Ektachrome."

"Are the viewers learning anything about Alaska?"

Ben Wade laughed. "I got a hot shot from my boss who wanted to know where I got those shots of green grass and flowers, and even those girls in bikinis down on Lake Spenard Beach. I told him I was secretly in Hawaii."

"The reactions toward soaring itself are very positive," said the NBC man. "There's been a run on soaring schools, I hear."

"Oh, the power of the press," breathed Jake Huggins.

"You're not kidding," said Ben Wade. "Remember that interview I did with the Aussie pilot who wiped out his club's ship? Well, my office tells me that contributions are still coming in, and his club ought to end up with enough dough to buy *two* new ships."

"That's good," said Jake. "I guess we're coming out ahead. I just hope it stays that way."

"What could happen?" asked Ben.

"Who knows? My old mammy taught me, always expect the worst and then no matter what happens, you won't be disappointed."

8

Amanda Webster found Barney Fields on the flight line, polishing his Skylark. He stood as she approached.

"You're early, sweetheart," he began.

"Don't sweetheart me, you bastard," she said.

He stiffened. "What's wrong?"

"You tell me," she said. "Tell me how a sky bum like Barney Fields gets three million dollars, and what he intends to do with it."

"Oh," he said. "Well, so I've got a little money. I earned it."

"And you'd like to run it up into ten million, or maybe twenty? Oh, Barney, we trusted you. And here you've been sneaking around behind our backs, making deals with the oil people."

"What's wrong with that?"

She stared at him defiantly. "You must think something's wrong, or you wouldn't have kept it so quiet."

"Not true. I learned a long time ago to keep my head down in the early stages of any deal, or the price has a habit of going up."

She threw a sheaf of business letters at him. "Well, here's your paperwork. You forgot to notify the post office when you moved out, and Lucille opened these by accident."

Barney scowled. "I suppose she read them by accident, too."

"That's not the point. I don't know what you did to her, but she delighted in nailing your hide to the wall. So much, that I fired her for being a snoop. But that doesn't alter the fact that you're not what you pretended. You're a god-damned carpetbagger, a spoiler. You want to suck what you can out of us and move on to your next target."

"That's not fair," said Barney. "I'm only setting up a supplementary air carrier—"

"And when would we have known about it? When you took in the pipeline equipment the rest of the carriers are boycotting until the environmental question has been settled?"

He turned away. "I'm sorry. This isn't what I intended."

"I'll bet it's not. Well, good luck, Barney. I'm only glad that Lucille was a snoop. She may have kept me from making a big mistake."

Barney turned back to answer, but by then she was already on her way back to her car.

JULY 6: *Free Distance Day*

1

IT WAS well after 7:00 A.M. before convection began. Three pilots had jumped the gun, tricked by wispy patches of cloud into believing that the first thermals of the day were starting to pop. In ignominy, they drifted back to the landing strip and took their places at the end of the takeoff line.

A small group of pilots waited near their planes.

"Enjoy your bleeding one-twelfth of a world's goal record," said Chet Cameron. "I aim to end up with the whole thing today."

"Don't be chicken, Chet," said Barney Fields. "Why not fly all the way to Toronto and be done with it?"

"The thought had occurred to me," said the English pilot. "But I decided the retrieve would take so long that I'd miss Discovery Day. No, I'll settle for Watson Lake. And while we're discussing half-measures, I can't conceal my disappointment in you, my boy. I thought you'd be going on down the Aleutian chain to Attu at least, if not all the way to Japan. Could it be you're lacking in good old American enterprise?"

Barney laughed. His head hurt. He had tried to call

Amanda several times last night, and when she did not answer, he'd called the bartender instead.

Over on the far side of the field, Jan Makula said, "We will win today. Take no chances. Keep in the air at any costs. That is the most important thing."

And, at the same time, Ron Smith was asking Renée Duval, "Did your ground crew add that front end ballast I suggested?"

"Certainly," she said. And thought, why should I take on more weight, you preposterous man? Your stalwart male pilots are so jealous of the advantage they believe my lesser load might bring, they have complained. Well, I will take on no weight just because you suggest it.

"I think I will try the dogleg," Wolf Lindner said to his wingman. "I can get the distance there. I am concerned about the landing spots. The maps show much rough terrain."

"Perhaps you should fly due east, with the majority of the planes," said the wingman. "There, at least, you will be more sure of retrieve."

"No," said the German. "Today I do not fly behind any man."

Seated in a camp chair near the radio shack, Major Anton Suslov studied the sky and thought, it is beginning. The wave is coming. I can sense it in the air. When the wind swings around tonight or in the morning, it will be here. I shall not take the good barograph today, the one that reads to seventy thousand feet. I dare not risk damaging it. All the others go off the paper at fifty thousand, and if I fly the wave tomorrow, I do not want to work that close to the edge of the trace. And I shall fly very carefully today. This would be no time to injure myself.

Inside the operations hangar, Ron Smith leaned against

the window, watching the anxious pilots pacing back and forth near their ships. Well, he thought, today will end the Championships, and end a few world's records too. And just in time. That front is moving, Harv tells me. It'll be through here late tonight. Then what? Can we count on weather like this every year? Or was this just a freak?

He smiled. I don't know, but if I'm still alive and flying this time next year, I plan to be up here giving it a whirl.

He heard a yell from the flight line. One of the pilots was pointing up into the northern sky. Yes, there they are, the first smudgy traces of cumulus.

At ten of eight in the morning, the Free Distance Day was off to its official beginning.

2

Barney Fields released below two thousand feet because he felt the bounce of a strong thermal and did not want the tug to take him past it. He waved his wings and dove off to the right to put a hundred foot notch in his barograph trace. All around him, the sky was coming to life with little puffs of cloud. Now he veered off to the southwest. He would have to be both cautious and daring today. Cautious to stay in the air, yet sufficiently daring to keep his groundspeed high enough to have a chance of covering that tremendous distance before running out of daylight.

His track would take him over Bearpaw, then down past Kankone Peak and the airstrip at Cripple Creek No. 1. Along the northeastern edge of the Alaska Range, past another landing strip at Farewell Lake. Then he would swing down the wide valley that runs due north and south, pointing the way to Ilamna Lake and the wide top of the Alaska Peninsula.

He flew with hands and feet off the controls for a moment to feel out the Skylark's trim. She was a little tail-heavy. That was a complaint most of the pilots had made, thanks to all the added-on communications gear. Had he turned on that damned transponder? Yes, by twisting his head, he could see its baleful red eye staring at him. And both barographs were ticking happily away.

The cumulus were forming all around him, so he could risk some speed. Drop the nose, listen to the airspeed build up. No pilot really needs to look at his airspeed indicator. The drumming of the air against the canopy tells me how fast I'm going. We're getting too mechanized, anyway. How about those guys who put a buzzer on their variometer, so they can tell when they're in lift without having to look at the instrument panel? If we're not careful, the sport will get so mechanical that the pilot will become just a lump of ballast for the ship to haul from one place to another. Ron Smith's fighting that trend, with his ban on radio traffic except for emergencies and retrieve. He laughed. That really shook the Foka Squadron up. He remembered reading about how, in the last Championship, the Polish fliers were issued weather instructions from the ground crew by radio, and how the sailplanes themselves were triangulated with radio direction finders. The pilots didn't even need to carry maps. That's going too far, he thought. I'm glad to see some move toward returning to basic pilotage.

A hawk came over to join Barney's thermal, and was obviously surprised when the sailplane continued to outclimb the bird. Barney smiled. He remembered the California pilot who had decided he would risk soaring over the elges of the Pacific Ocean.

"Why not?" asked the pilot. "Sea gulls do. If they can find lift, so can I. I've already been flying with them off Torrey Pines, and in any thermal worth its name, I can actually outclimb a gull."

The same pilot, a week later, sat in the hangar coffeeshop and glumly related the results of his experiment.

"It worked fine," he said. "I picked up this big bastard of a gull, and he did a few figure eights over the beach. So did I, and it was mighty fine lift. I figured I had it knocked. Then he zipped out on a little excursion over the waves. My heart was in my throat, but I followed him. By God, there was lift galore out there, and my white-feathered friend led me right into it. Well, our game went on for an hour or so, and my gull never let me down, and I got braver and braver. Pretty soon we were out further and further. I had the world by the tail. If there was a scrap of lift to be had, my buddy found it. Fnally he led me way out, a mile or so, but I wasn't worried. Then the lift dropped off, and I found myself in zero sink, and pretty soon the old red pellet came up in the tube and I said to my seagull friend, okay, old buddy, you'd better get us out of here." He gulped down his coffee. "Do you know what that feathered bastard did? He headed back toward shore, all right. Flapping his goddamned wings!"

Well, thought Barney, there'll be no wing-flapping today. The flatlands slid by under the Skylark's nose. The fluffy bit of string taped to it lay straight back toward the center of the canopy. Barney smiled. He'd spent hundreds of dollars on sophisticated instruments, but he could not bear to part from the little bit of string that told him that he was flying true, neither slipping nor skidding.

Suddenly, his eyes clouded. He felt weary. Tired already? That's not good. There's a full day of flying ahead. Why did you have to be such an idiot? Staying up late and drinking isn't the best training for a distance attempt.

Watch the altitude. It's time for another thermal elevator ride. Then make the dash between clouds and find another thermal. Keep that up for eighteen hours and you'll put your name in the record books.

The slipstream drummed against his Skylark, and it was a soothing, almost melodic lullaby.

3

That's Buffalo Center down there, thought Chet Cameron. Good show. The wind's not behind me yet, but I really don't need it now, the way those lovely clouds are forming. Later in the day, I'll start going up into them when it's worth it to fight for the extra altitude. But I can't complain now, with cloud base at six-five hundred indicated altitude, and what looks like a cloud street forming down through the Tanana Valley. Wouldn't *that* be loverly? Roaring along at sixty-five under a cloud street; that's my idea of a pleasant morning in Alaska.

Ah, would the blokes from the Lasham Gliding Association ever find this a delight. Much as we love our sceptered isles, it's not to be denied that they're just too damned small to provide much in the way of distance. Precious few distance diamonds were ever picked up there. Unless, naturally, you just happened to get "blown off course" and drift over the channel to France. That's happening more and more often, now that the word's gone round that the worst you can expect is a tongue-lashing from the Air Ministry.

Do I have a chance to win this year? Not too good. The French girl will have to go down with low mileage, and I'd have to beat out the Foka Squadron. Fat chance. They've got their technique down cold. Can't begrudge them, though. We could do the same, if we wanted to. It's just not my idea of what it's all about.

It'll be great to see the wife and the nippers again. It feels as if I've been away forever. Perhaps I won't wait for the RAF shuttle at the end of the week. Maybe I can talk myself aboard the BOAC polar flight, seeing as how they usually go out half-empty anyway. It'll bear thinking about.

The silver Dart 27 turned into another thermal and corkscrewed itself up into the intense blueness over Buffalo Center. Chet saw his lift surge to seven hundred feet a minute just below cloud base and instantly decided to continue on up into the cumulus. "What the hell?" he said out loud. "Got to lose my cherry sometime today anyway."

4

Staff Sergeant Alvin Handley sat in his cramped radar room aboard a huge Air Force plane circling over central Alaska at fifty thousand feet. There were three radar scopes before him, set to different ranges. They were adjusted to receive the signals from the transponders mounted in each sailplane.

"Look at that," said the sergeant. "Those bastards are scattering all over the map."

This was not precisely true, although there were certainly enough blips spreading out in various directions from Fairbanks to give that impression. Most of the planes were heading east, toward Whitehorse. Several, deciding that the weather forecast was in error about the winds swinging around in the afternoon, were taking advantage of the northeast wind to head almost due west, hoping for a flight to Scammon Bay or St. Michael, on the west coast of the state.

Only two blips had broken away from the crowd. One had turned around the Alaska Range and was now well down along the valley between Halfway Mountain and the Bonanza Hills. Reading the initials "B.F.," the sergeant said, "That's Barney Fields. He's the nut that got this whole thing started."

"Well, speaking of nuts," said Airman First Class Sam Meyer, "take a look at this other one. He's right there in the middle of the goddamned mountains. See? Just east of Peters Dome."

Identifying the transponder signal, the sergeant said, "It's that Russian, the cosmonaut."

"And we let him fly around Alaska on his own?" said Meyer. "That's real heavy thinking."

"What do you want from me?" asked the sergeant. "I just work here. And so do you, remember? So get your ass back on that RDF. If we lose any of these birds, Russian or not, the Captain has promised to chew a neat ring around our asses and let the middle part fall out."

"Yes sir, sergeant," said Airman First Class Meyer.

5

It is not too bad, thought Anton Suslov. Keep in mind that no matter how much trouble you encounter here in the rocks, you can always turn away and glide downhill to the valley.

I will continue down this route, then turn west over toward Kuskokwim Bay, near the Ahklun Mountains. That will give me more than five hundred and fifty miles if I make it to my goal of Bethel, and there are several landing strips indicated on the map.

Meanwhile, he thought, as his wing slid just above the jutting peaks, it is interesting to taste these mountains. If the wave comes, I will be in practice.

He smiled. There is no need to be this low. But these mountains are just like a woman. Even though it is too soon to take them to my bed, I cannot keep my hands away from them. I cannot resist the sly little smiles and the whispered promises and the furtive taste of early kisses.

Enough foolishness. Turn away from the naked rock and find a thermal to take you out of this valley.

6

Renée Duval found herself trapped in a bowl-like valley just north of Mineral Point. What few feet of lift she found on the good side of the bowl were immediately lost when she circled to the bad side.

How did I ever let myself be drawn into this treacherous place? It was madness to believe that the wind blowing down the valley would bring me through the Mentasta Mountains. I thought I had a straight glide to the Alaska-Yukon border, where the Alaska Highway crosses from Canada at Border City. Instead, here I am scraping along a few feet above the unfriendly rocks, barely managing to stay in the air. And I am too long into my flight to hope for a tow back to Fairbanks and a second start. If I go down here, that is the end of my chances today . . . and the finish for me in the Championships.

Shall I radio the tug before I get so low that the mountains may block my signal?

No! I will be sitting on the ground before I admit defeat.

Wait . . . was that last circle a little better? It is hard to tell, when you're dealing in tens of feet instead of hundreds.

Damn this valley! It will not have me! I have never submitted in my life. Not to a man, not to God, and certainly not to blind nature!

As if in answer to her problem, a tiny flutter of rising air broke free from the valley floor and nibbled at her wings. With breathless concentration, she managed to capture it, bringing the green pellet up in its tube.

Now the Edelweiss was rising instead of merely holding its own, and foot by infuriating foot, the valley walls began to fall beneath its wings.

7

The middle of the day is a sleepy time and, to Barney Fields, it was more so. He cruised slowly over hundreds of small lakes where the Alaska Peninsula joins the main body of the state. Concentration had become more and more difficult. Often, he lost his thermals completely, and had to backtrack to center them again.

Try a little more coffee.

Any more coffee and my back teeth will float away. This would be the day that I forgot to bring a plastic bottle!

Well, one thing's sure, Barney old boy. You can't land with a full bladder. That's a sure way to end up in the hospital, bursting the stupid thing.

He grinned. I'll use the coffee flask. It already tastes like piss anyway.

Center that thermal! You're flying like a beginner!

Barney took another swig of the bitter coffee.

I should have gotten more sleep last night.

What the hell kind of excuse is that? Lindbergh flew two days and a night to get to Paris, and he didn't have any sleep the night before, either.

Yeah, but he wasn't drinking martinis.

That just goes to show you how Lindbergh was a little smarter than you. Now get with it.

8

Wolf Lindner found the going easier now. The last ten miles had been frightening. He had been turning south, along the eastern edge of the St. Elias Mountains, in Yukon Territory, when the turbulence increased to the point where his feet were being thrown free of the rudder pedals and barking his shins on the bottom of the instrument panel. His head smashed against the canopy of the Ka-20 several times so hard that he saw stars. Finally, he stuffed his flight cap with the packet of tissues he'd brought along and while his head did not stop hitting the plastic, at least now it did not hurt so much.

Something strange is happening to the air. I am not at all sure I like it. I think perhaps a stream of warm air is coming up from the Pacific Ocean and colliding with the colder flow out of the north, and we are getting a wind shear. If this keeps up, the thermals may vanish altogether.

But no, apparently it was only a local condition. Because I have been able to fly at best lift-over-drag speed toward Skagway, and the turbulence is decreasing.

Wolf had not declared a goal before takeoff. He did not want to be influenced by any predetermined destination. He was going for the best total distance, and it did not matter where he found it. His instincts told him that he would do best flying southeast. But if conditions changed, he would turn straight inland without a qualm, trusting to his own skill and to the Air National Guard.

9

The Foka Squadron sailed blithely over Burwash Landing in the Yukon Territory. The fifteen-thousand-foot peak of Mountain Wood was behind them. The Polish fliers had a comfortable four thousand feet over terrain, for an absolute altitude of perhaps nine thousand feet above sea level.

One of the pilots had declared Whitehorse as a goal, but it would only be taken if conditions beyond Whitehorse were too risky to expect to get much farther. Extra points for another forty or fifty miles were more important than winning the goal record.

Jan Makula ached to speak to his teammates over the radio, to tell them that he sensed the wind was coming about and that they should not waste too much time climbing for altitude because soon they would have the wind directly behind, helping them. But it was too risky. He did not know how sensitive the radio monitoring system was, but it was certainly not worth being penalized to find out.

10

And a fond farewell to Whitehorse, grinned Chet Cameron, squinting down at the village. What the hell time is it, anyway? After eight! No wonder the old tum-tum's growling. It was a silly move to put the sandwiches back there with the barographs. To get them, I'll have to unharness, twist around, and trust the bloody ship to fly itself while I scramble around in the baggage compartment. Let the old gut growl. Another hundred miles . . . say four hours . . . and I'll be on the ground and stuff myself with a great beefsteak.

He sat up straighter. Or will I? Where the hell will I find a pub open in this wilderness?

That tears it. I'm going to get those sandwiches before my stomach digests itself.

Chet unsnapped his shoulder harness and seat belt, then let go of the controls to see what the Dart would do. It should still be in good trim, he thought. I haven't given her any bashing around recently.

Yes, her nose drops, and she dives a little until she gets up excess air speed, then the nose comes up and she slows down, getting slower and slower until she loses flying speed and she stalls out. But she stalls straight ahead, like she should, and as she falls, the nose drops and the whole procedure is repeated. Any good ship ought to do the same, just porpoising safely through the air with no hand at the controls. But if she's out of trim, she can go mean on you, dropping off on one wing and creating a spin condition before you know it.

Chet twisted around and rummaged around for the paper bag of sandwiches. Careful, don't bugger about with the miserable barographs. You don't want them to go on the fritz and make all this work for nothing. Ah, here's the sandwich bag.

He fastened himself into the plane again before opening the bag.

Ah, he thought. One thing about the American mess hall, the boys there really know how to make a peanut butter and jelly sandwich.

11

I'll just close my eyes long enough to count to ten, thought Barney Fields.

One, two, three. . . .

What are you doing, you idiot?

I only wanted to rest my eyes.

You only want to kill yourself! Look at the airspeed. You're in a spiral dive and you're up to 115 miles an hour. If you can't fly this thing any more, land it. That's Port Heiden down there to the right. You're halfway down the Peninsula. Call it a day. It's almost 10:00 P.M. You'll run out of thermals pretty soon anyway. Settle for seven hundred miles.

I'm awake. I'm awake.

Sure you are. Your head is almost as asleep as your ass. Turn back. There's a safe landing strip over there on the other side of the river. Put her on the ground, then you can lie down and sleep. This is crazy. You've already beaten Al Parker. What do you want, blood?

Those boys going down into the Yukon may get eight hundred miles. I've got to beat them, too.

You don't know that they made it.

I don't know they didn't, either.

Then do something to keep awake. This is a very forgiving ship. It will fly itself. But not when you're leaning all over the controls and snoring.

I'll think about Amanda. She's a real woman. Nothing phony about her. She did everything for real. She ate steak like she meant it, just like she drove her car and made love.

She also sent you to the cleaners when she found out you weren't Mr. Straight-Arrow.

I can fix that up.

Lot's of luck. Maybe you'd better think about the French girl instead.

Isn't she something? I wonder what the hell she was up to?

Maybe she wanted to get you and Suslov at each other's throats.

She wouldn't. I'd break her goddamned neck.

First, you'd better avoid breaking your own. That ridge up ahead might be nice for some slope soaring, but only if you get the Skylark out of this dive before you clobber into it. Gentle back pressure on the stick. Don't peel off the wings. How are you doing, old buddy?

I'm wide awake. No fooling. The first stop's Scotch

Cap. And then we'll get out the Royal Mounties and locate Amanda.

Good idea, but the Mounties are over in Canada. In Alaska, they have sheriffs, forest rangers, things like that. But I'm glad to see that old fighting spirit back in your eye. Now, make sure to get enough altitude and–

Shut up. I'm flying this plane. I'm in charge here, now. You can go to sleep if you want. And thanks for waking me up.

Don't mention it. See you down at Scotch Cap.

12

Bethel, Alaska, first became famous for the un-Alaskan fact that, with more than a thousand souls in residence, this Moravian missionary center does not have a single bar. This fact distressed Major Anton Suslov considerably when he was borne down to the center of town in triumph–and then offered a glass of iced tea. Luckily, a less than temperate doctor rescued him and invited Suslov home for a few hot toddies while the Russian awaited the arrival of his tow plane.

"These missionaries do a hell of a lot of good," said the doctor. "I only wish they had a more liberal attitude about the fruit of the vine. Half of the time, we doctors are reduced to drinking our medicinal alcohol."

"How many doctors is that?" asked Suslov. "I would not think a small town such as this would be overrun with medical men."

"You'd be surprised. We had ten at last count. Of course, we don't just take care of the town. This is where we have the field hospital for the natives. I guess we serve some twelve thousand people from sixty or seventy villages."

Suslov shook his head. "That's amazing."

"It's a crime the way these people were ignored for so long when Alaska was still a territory. I wonder how some of the honored men in Washington sleep at nights, knowing they have a hundred thousand deaths on their consciences."

"In what way?"

"Until we had the hospital, all we could do was portage back into those cruddy villages and try to treat those poor kids, crippled by TB, and try to cheer up their parents—who usually had the disease themselves. Next trip in, I'd write out the kids' death certificates."

"I thought tuberculosis was a disease of the past."

"Not up here. A few years ago, six out of every hundred natives had it. We used to get the Air Force to fly rescue missions, to bring the children in for treatment. Those roundups saved thousands of lives. And don't you know some loudmouth in Congress raised hell because we were 'wasting' the taxpayers' money? Our friendly neighborhood airlines didn't help, either. They figured they should get a slice of the pie. They couldn't seem to get it through their heads that *nobody* was getting paid." The doctor sighed and poured another drink. "Now I suppose you'll go back to Moscow and spread the word that we're mistreating our natives. Well, what the hell? I always spoke the truth up to now, and I'm too old to change."

"Do not be disturbed about what I might say," said Suslov. "I am not interested in propaganda. I am impressed by your honesty, and what you are doing here. Nothing will change that."

They sat quietly, drinking, until a knock at the door told Suslov that his retrieve crew had arrived.

13

Shortly after midnight, the few planes still left in the sky began falling out of it like silver hail. All lift was gone, as the ships went into their final glide.

Wolf Lindner went down east of Juneau, near Telegraph Creek. He would score just over seven hundred miles for the day's flight.

One by one, the Foka Squadron landed in the mountains between Whitehorse and Watson Lake, along the Moose River. Their distances averaged almost eight hundred miles for each ship. While they waited for their retrieve planes to arrive, Jan Makula uncorked a secret bottle of potato vodka, and the four pilots each had a healthy belt.

Renée Duval fell twelve miles short of Watson Lake and sat in the long shadow of her Edelweiss and smiled coldly without humor as she looked up and saw Chet Cameron's Dart on its final glide, with five thousand feet of altitude, more than enough to reach the field at Watson Lake.

In fact, Chet had enough altitude left for a triumphant pass over the airstrip before landing. His retrieve team was already waiting when he coasted off the runway, unhooked the canopy and stood up.

"Gor blimey," he said in broad cockney, "me arse has been asleep for the past hundred miles. Where's the crapper?"

14

Barney Fields clawed his way around the upwind side of Unimak Island. All thermal lift was gone and the ridge lift was weakening. The aircraft clock on the Skylark's instrument panel read ten after two. Although there was less than fifty miles to his goal, he knew that he would have to be very lucky to make it. The air outside the sailplane had become ominously still, and he did not have enough altitude left to set up any kind of final glide.

He beat along the very edge of the mountainous coastline, praying that the offshore wind would not stop, at least for the next few minutes. He was making good groundspeed, but the ridge ended just ahead, and then he would have to leave its safety and plunge into the unknown.

Awareness of his body had left him a long time ago. Nor did he make any pretense at precision flying. It was too much to ask of his tattered senses. Just keeping the Skylark in the air and penetrating toward the goal was enough.

Barney could not remember a time when he had not been flying this sailplane. The past was a dim, gray vagueness. He knew only that it was very necessary that he keep the Skylark in the air until he ran out of land and faced the sea. Then, and only then, could he land and find sleep.

He left the ridge and plunged across a valley full of sinking air. He arrived at another ridge with barely enough altitude to crawl up its side, one wing only feet above the wind-torn vegetation. There was not much lift, but it was enough. He forced himself to keep the wing tip close to the ridge. Once, it clipped the branches of a small tree, and he was tossed away from the slope and immediately lost what little lift there was. He dove the Skylark violently, then yanked back on the stick and converted the extra speed of the dive into altitude. Now he would either find the lift again, or he would stall out at the top of the arc and plunge down the rugged hill.

The Skylark's wings tasted the delight of lift again, and man and machine flew toward the distant sea where the Bering Sea meets the Pacific Ocean through the narrow Unimak Passage.

Then suddenly he was flying south, according to his compass, and he saw only blue water on three sides, with the island to his left, and he knew that he was at the very tip of the large island that touched the Alaska Peninsula. This was Scotch Cap, and naturally the bluffs ran right down to the surf-torn beach and there was nowhere within reach to land. He tried to turn back up to the airstrip at Cape Sarichef, but the relentless wind pressed him into the unforgiving cliffs. The wing of the Skylark sliced through green bushes and tipped against the harsh rocks and, with a whirling vertigo that was almost pleasant, Barney felt himself and the damaged sailplane tumbling toward the sea far below.

15

As the short Alaskan night came on, the retrieve pilot of Major Anton Suslov's L-16 looked out and said, "Hey, how about that? Mount McKinley's wearing a cap."

Suslov, half-dozing, lifted his head and stared at the huge mountain just fifty miles away. A smooth, lens-shaped cloud had settled down almost on the very peak. It was still small, but growing.

Yes, the wave was beginning.

JULY 7: *The Rest Day*

1

"I WILL kill you!" screamed Renée Duval. Her fingernails reached for Anton Suslov's eyes.

He laughed and held her wrists.

"Be gentle now," he said. "Your delicate condition, my darling."

"How dare you tell lies about me?"

"What lies?"

"These!" she cried, holding up the front page of the Fairbanks *News-Miner*.

"RUSSIAN PILOT SECRETLY WED TO FRENCH AVIATRIX," read the banner headline. And, in smaller type: "*Hints Bride is Flying for Two.*"

"Am I to understand," said Suslov, "that you do not find the prospect of marriage with me appealing?"

"I will wait until you are asleep," Renée promised grimly. "Then I will take a scissor and gouge your eyes out!"

"Be patient for another few days," Suslov said. "Then you may have your freedom."

"But why did you do it, Anton? Everybody must be laughing about it. Laughing at me. This story has gone around the world by now. And it is not true, none of it is true. Why?"

"Perhaps I do not care to share you with the American. I doubt if I will have to, after today."

"Stupid! There was nothing between us."

"Merely what Barney would call a one-night stand? Well, now I am sure."

Renée said, "You are stupid, Anton."

Suslov frowned. "I hope he is not hurt too badly. Why no tears over his crash?"

"They are flying him in this morning. He cannot be injured seriously."

"Still, you ought to have some feeling for him. For old times' sake?"

"I do not recognize the past," she said.

"You are an amazing woman, Renée. Well, be patient. In another week, your unfortunate marriage will be forgotten. In the meanwhile, my dear, please do be careful. The little one, you know."

"And what will you be doing? I suppose you are still going to try to reach the top of your insane wave."

"Later in the afternoon, yes. The mountain is almost ready for me." He looked at his watch. "We will have lunch, and then I will go."

"Good," she said. "Then I will be a widow by sundown."

"That is not a thing to jest about," he said.

"Why not? Are you superstitious, Anton? A famous cosmonaut, scientist, sophisticated man of the world. And still a peasant under it all?" She laughed harshly.

"There is still a little peasant in all of us," he said. "And a good thing, too. It is the only thing that keeps us in touch with the earth. I have learned that the city is a madhouse, and as in any madhouse, all the inmates are convinced they alone are sane. But when a man still has a little peasant in his bones, he has not lost rapport with reality."

"Oh, spare me your homespun philosophies," cried Renée Duval. "Go off and kill yourself on your stupid mountain while I send some telegrams. You have no idea how much trouble this joke of yours will cause me."

"My pleasure," said Anton Suslov.

"Get out!"

"Gladly. But when I come back from Mount McKinley, I will return to you. After all, a husband has his rights."

"I'll see you in hell first!" she screamed, slamming the door.

2

The official results of the competition were posted in the Operations Hangar.

Winning Teams

1. Poland
2. U.S.A.
3. Great Britain
4. Switzerland
5. West Germany

Winning Pilots

	PILOT	NATION	SAILPLANE	TOTAL SCORE
1.	R. Duval	France	Edelweiss C-30	2130
2.	C. Cameron	Gr. Britain	Dart 27	2092
3.	B. Fields	U.S.A.	Skylark 12	1975
4.	J. Makula	Poland	Foka 14	1921
5.	A. Suslov	U.S.S.R.	KAI-24	1913

Casualties were light. Two ships had been totally destroyed—the Australian Boomerang and Barney Fields' Skylark. In neither case had the crash been caused by any special hazard of Alaskan terrain or weather. Four other sailplanes had been damaged in rough landings. One, the new French ship, the Libelle Supreme, wiped out its landing gear in a wild groundloop that would have destroyed a more conventional plane. But, with her all-fiberglass body, the Libelle survived with only minor scratches to the airframe.

One pilot from India had landed on a glacier during the Free Distance Day, and had not taken proper precautions against the glare. His eyes were now heavily bandaged, with a bad case of snow blindness. Another pilot who had made an almost-impossible safe landing in a rock-filled valley, got up on a rock to signal his retrieve plane, fell off, and broke his ankle.

Wolf Lindner had developed a splitting headache from bouncing off his own canopy in the heavy turbulence near Skagway. He was glum about not placing in the top five. His team had finished fifth and he, personally, was number eight. He admitted privately that was probably where he deserved to be, considering the caliber of the flying in the Championships.

Over lunch, Bill Webster looked at his wife, who picked at her plate.

Finally, he said, "The word is, he isn't hurt too bad."

"I know," she said. She put down her napkin. "Bill, I'm sorry. I have to go down and meet the plane."

Quietly, he said, "It's your decision, Amanda."

Tears sprang to her eyes, but she did not answer. She kissed his cheek and hurried from the room.

Webster stared down at his unfinished meal. Then he swept the plate from the table.

"Goddamnit!" he said. "Why did it have to be Barney?"

3

The reports that Barney's Skylark had "fallen into the sea" were more dramatic than accurate. Actually, the sailplane fell into the *edge* of the sea, in less than a foot of gentle surf and, although it took almost an hour for rescuers to arrive and climb down the cliffs, Barney was never in any real danger of drowning. In fact, he was still sitting in the cockpit, sound asleep, when help arrived.

With the incredible luck of the very young, or the very drunk, Barney had been bounced around in the shattered wreckage of his Skylark in a state of semiconsciousness that left him limp and virtually immune to injury. He escaped the dangerous spinal compresion that can occur in a flat-flying attitude crash, because the Skylark had cartwheeled down the rocky slope. Each impact tore off more wing surface, and slowed the descent, and then to complete Barney's good fortune, the fuselage landed tail first, so that the fragile tail surfaces ate up more of the kinetic energy. This was the best position for the pilot, since the seat back cushioned his body for the final impact.

Taken to the small hospital at Fort Randall for a checkup, Barney frustrated the doctors by sleeping through it all, including the X-rays.

4

Major Anton Suslov seated the two barographs carefully in the special compartment in the rear of his KAI-24. Both were fully wound and had been sealed by an official observer.

"We will wait for the wave condition to develop a little more," he told his tow pilot. "The reports indicate the lenticular cloud is developing nicely downwind of the peak. The wind is strengthening, and I think if we enter the wave around 1400 hours, it will be just about right."

"Don't get too ambitious," warned the tow pilot. "You only need forty-eight thousand feet, tops. Don't try to eat the whole sky."

"Never fear," said Suslov. "I am only concerned with being the one to beat Paul Bikle, not becoming the first sailplane to go into orbit. I will be breathing pure oxygen from fifteen thousand feet, and I will break off the flight at forty-eight thousand no matter now good the remaining lift."

"Where do you want to enter the wave? Around six thousand feet?"

"Lower," said the major. "Getting the highest absolute altitude isn't enough. I've got to make more than forty-one thousand feet altitude *gain*, or the job is only half done."

"That means you'll have to release around four thousand feet indicated altitude."

"Is that possible?"

"It is if I drop you down in the valley, over Gold Creek. Ground level there is only five hundred feet or so. If you let go at twenty-five hundred, you'll be two thousand feet above terrain, and if you get your forty-eight thousand, you'll gain over forty-five thousand feet. But that means you'll have to fight your way up the slopes to pick up the wave, and what's more, you'll come pretty close to the roll cloud. You might even go into it. That's not such good news."

"In that case, we'd better plan on being over the valley an hour earlier. Maybe we'd better start now."

"Okay. And major"

"Yes?"

"Take my advice. Wear some warm socks."

5

"Well, Wolf old man," said Chet Cameron, "the Foka Squadron beat us out again."

"I expected it," said Wolf Lindner. "Their teamwork was superb."

"What frosts me," said Chet, "is that the little buggers seem to *enjoy* it so much. I've been taught all my life that regimentation is stifling, that it's bad, and that it certainly isn't enjoyable. So where do our Polish friends get off parading around with those shit-eating grins?"

"It is enjoyable to win," said the German. "Or haven't you noticed?"

"Indeed I have," said Chet. "Sorry about your own bad luck. As for me, I was lucky."

"May it always continue," said Wolf. "Now what do you plan? Are you going to try the McKinley wave this afternoon? I understand this will be our only chance. It will be washed away by the wind shift tomorrow."

"I think I may have a go at it," said Chet. "The Lord only knows my behind is starting to mold itself to fit the fuselage of my Dart, but I imagine I can stand another three or four hours, especially if it could complete my diamond badge. Of course, I'd better stay out of Suslov's way."

"I am afraid for him," said Wolf. "A man cannot survive long at the heights he plans."

"Well, Bikle survived right enough to forty-six thousand. And Suslov is younger than Bikle was in 1961. I think he's got a good shot at the thing, if the wave goes high enough and his luck holds out."

"Yes," said Wolf. "Luck has a good deal to do with it."

6

As the Air Force jet taxied down the runway at Eielson, Barney Fields said, "Stop over there, will you, Lieutenant? I want to talk with one of the glider pilots."

"I've never seen so many weird looking planes in my life," said the jet pilot. "Gliders? Is that what you cracked up?"

"One and the same," said Barney.

"What the hell were you doing off the tip of Unimak Island in a *glider*?"

"When I find out, I'll let you know," said Barney. "I'll get out here. Many thanks for the ride."

"My pleasure," said the Air Force pilot. "Watch yourself, don't get too close to the jet intakes."

"Right," said Barney. He climbed down and trotted over to the KAI-24, where Major Anton Suslov was completing his cockpit check.

"Barney!" said the Russian, grabbing Barney's hand. "I am glad to see you're still in one piece."

"I lucked out," said Barney. "But I did it. I got my goal. We haven't put it on the spherical globe yet, but I figure it'll go just over a thousand miles. Lucky I had two barographs. The ink trace got spoiled in the water, but the one that punches on foil is okay."

"Good job," said Suslov.

"Are you going for the wave?"

"Yes. The weather people say it is splendid. Perhaps I will have a surprise for your friend, Mr. Bikle."

"I hope so, Anton. Give it hell." Barney helped the wingman close the canopy. Suslov waved as the sailplane rolled down the runway behind the tow plane.

Barney turned, and found himself being kissed on the mouth by Amanda Webster.

"Now that's a welcome," he said.

7

"The hell with those crazy bastards," said Ben Wade. "This is my day off, by God, and I am going to sit here with my shoes off and drink good bourbon until I forget I ever saw a sailplane." The cameraman made good his boast by half draining his glass. "What's the matter with them, are they all mental cases? They flew halfway to hell and back yesterday, and sat up half the night in the retrieve planes, and now here they are dashing over to Mount McKinley for a little recreational flying!"

"They're nuts all right," Jake Huggins agreed. "That's why I love them, bless their little pointed heads. How long is it since you did something just for the plain, simple joy of *doing* it? Hell, that's the only thing I hate about running a newspaper. There's nothing in the world I can do without my mind twisting it around to turn it into copy. If I go on vacation and catch the biggest damned salmon in the whole state of Alaska, can I hold it to my secret heart? Hell no, I turn it into a feature article, and that makes it into *work*. And I bet you're the same. You never go anywhere without that movie camera, not even to the john."

"Well, you never know when something's going to happen," said Wade.

"That's just what I said," Jake answered. "You're on duty twenty-four hours a day, and so am I. But those jokers up there are cruising around in the clouds mainly because they love it."

Glumly, Ben Wade said, "I heard from the lab quality control boys. They haven't been cutting my original film. But they liked my Boomerang crash sequence so much they put it on the air without making a safety print, and naturally the goddamned film chain projector put a big scratch right down the middle."

"That's too bad."

"I think I can get the scratch buffed out," said Wade. "They can do great things today in reconditioning film. But that sequence would have to be one of the key ones in the whole film. I'd hate to lose it."

"See what I mean? On duty twenty-four hours a day. Now, me, I'm just sitting here thinking of sticking a case of beer in a mountain stream and just wasting away the whole week-end fly casting. I'm so lazy that I may not even use a hook."

"You'll probably catch something anyway," said Ben Wade. "Then you'll have to write an article about it."

"Why don't you take a flying you-know-what at a rolling doughnut?"

"After you," said the cameraman.

The two men sat in the warm Officer's Club, dozing. It was a nice day to be warm and comfortable and do absolutely nothing.

8

Major Anton Suslov released two thousand feet above the small village of Hurricane in the valley that runs between the Alaska Range and the Talkeetna Mountains. Mount McKinley, flanked by Mount Hather and Mount Silver Throne, hung over him in the early afternoon sky. He dove the sailplane a hundred feet to put a good notch on the barograph trace, and then began working the lift for all it was worth. He would be very happy to gain enough altitude to dive under the vicious roll cloud. If he could turn altitude into speed, he might get through the area of maximum turbulence without too much trouble.

This day he would learn if his skill and his ship were up to the task. The sailplane was in top shape. All instruments had been double-checked. The two barographs were ticking away in their compartment, carefully taped down to keep them in place. Both oxygen cylinders were full, and the mask and regulator were working perfectly. His altitude suit was laced up so tightly that it hurt, and he had taken the tow pilot's advice about warm socks.

Now he could see the rolling, tossing bottomside of the roll cloud. It was like looking into an angry cauldron of bubbling water. The first gusts hit him, and the wings of the sailplane flexed. The variometer registered down air.

Then he hit violent updrafts. The variometer showed him

that he was going up at almost two thousand feet a minute. This isn't good. The roll cloud is sucking me in.

Suslov put the sailplane's nose down and opened up his dive brakes. The rate of ascent slowed, but still continued at six hundred feet a minute. This is no good! To hell with the dive brakes.

He released them and tried to fall out of the rising torrent of air. But now its velocity increased beyond his ability to penetrate it.

"Alpha Sierra Tug, this is Alpha Sierra Air," he radioed. "I'm being pulled into the roll cloud. I will stay on my northwesterly course and hope to fly out within a few minutes. Stand by for a retrieve if my plane breaks up and I have to use the parachute. Over."

"Roger, Alpha Sierra," said the tow pilot.

The ground below vanished in the swirling mists of the cloud's base. The air became very rough. Suslov fought the controls. First one wing was down, then the other. He was conscious of being tossed violently from side to side.

The lift dropped off somewhat, but continued at around three hundred feet a minute. Rain drummed on the wing surfaces and cascaded over the canopy, blotting out visibility. Suslov was strictly on instruments now, watching the artificial horizon and the ball and bank indicator to be sure he did not let the KAI-24 slip into a spiral dive. Meanwhile, he continued trying to fly along his planned course, although the compass was swinging wildly.

He felt the first watering in his mouth and a constriction of his stomach that warned of airsickness.

That will never do, he thought, setting his will power against the sensations. What is my altitude now? Almost ten thousand feet. The roll cloud has added more than four thousand feet to my climb, and now if only I can get out of its monstrous interior, I will be in good shape for the wave.

At that very moment, the sailplane fell out of the cloud's side and Anton Suslov rejoiced to see the white marbled sides of Mount McKinley straight ahead and, high above his canopy, the incredibly beautiful swirls of a lenticular cloud, visible evidence of a powerful standing wave.

9

"Barney," said Bill Webster, "why don't you and I take a little sailplane ride?"

Barney Fields stared at the mayor of Fairbanks. "Why?" he asked. "I thought you might be more interested in giving me a rap on the jaw."

Webster shook his head. "You know that's not the way."

"Maybe not," said Barney, "but if our positions were reversed, I think I'd give it a try."

"Let's try it my way," said Webster. "You're pretty proud of your flying. Well, buddy, I used to whip a few around up there, too."

"Power's different from soaring," said Barney.

"So you keep telling me."

"Bill, I'm sorry the way things have turned out, but–"

"What's the matter, Fields? Afraid to fly with an ex-jet jockey?"

"I just don't see the point in it," said Barney.

"You will," Webster told him.

10

Major Anton Suslov found himself in an area of violent sink, his plane headed straight for the mountain wall. He lowered the ship's nose and watched altitude unwind. He bit his lip. I must find the wave soon. If I get too low, I will be forced back through the roll cloud again, and I do not think either my ship or my stomach are up to it.

A savage bump announced the end of his descent as he ran into a wall of rising air that seemed as solid as the rocks themselves. As the thermal lifted him toward the mighty lenticular cloud above, he saw that he was at 6750 feet. The lift began at four hundred feet a minute and soon climbed to more than six hundred feet a minute. As he passed twelve thousand feet, the turbulence ceased and he knew that he was in the wave proper, riding its very edge like a surfer on the rim of the sea. At fifteen thousand feet he slipped on the oxygen mask and felt his head become clearer as the bitingly cold oxygen fed into his lungs.

Now we are on our way, he thought, as the altimeter crept past seventeen thousand feet. He was now rising at over a thousand feet a minute, but the lift was so smooth that had it not been for the instruments, he would have sworn he was sitting on a quiet field somewhere. At nineteen thousand feet his canopy was completely iced up, and he could hear hail hitting the wings. The incredibly smooth lift continued, and all he had to do to hold it was keep the ship's nose down and fly directly into the wind with enough speed to neutralize its velocity. The clock face variometer registered more than two thousand feet a minute, and the green pellet was jammed in the top of its tube.

Is that altimeter sticking? Yes, it is. Tap it. The reading was 24,500 feet, and after the tap it shot up another thousand feet. Give yourself more oxygen. You need more at this height. Suslov moved his toes. Despite the heavy socks, they were becoming numb. Tap the altimeter again. It is still lagging. Over thirty thousand now, and both variometers are off the scale. Who knows how fast I am rising? The hail is heavier now and, yes, the canopy is frozen solid and starting to distintegrate.

The intensely cold air rushed into the cockpit and tore at his face, at his clothing, rushing up his sleeves. But still he kept tapping the altimeter and watching his airspeed.

Keep it at a steady sixty miles an hour. That seems to be the right speed to stay with the leading edge of the wave. I am completely blind now. The ice on the canopy must be an inch thick. But still this superb plane flies as if it were only a quiet summer day.

Suslov shivered constantly now, and his stomach felt very cold and empty. His gloved hands were numb with the cold, and every time he tapped the altimeter he felt that his fingers might fall off.

How long have we been at forty thousand feet? That is not possible. We must still be climbing. But the needle does not move. It must be frozen. We are going up at least two thousand feet a minute. So I will continue to climb for another four minutes, and that will give me a safe forty-nine thousand feet for the world's record.

But you only need forty-eight thousand!

I know, but who knows how high I really am, with the damned stupid altimeter asleep?

Beneath his chin, unseen, ice formed on the regulator of his oxygen mask.

You are falling asleep! Pinch yourself! You must not let the altitude confuse you or muddle your brain. You are not making a moon walk now, there is no backup team in the command module.

Center that ball bank! Why are you turning?

How many minutes more must I climb? Is it three? Or five?

Suslov, you are drunk. Turn on more oxygen.

He twisted the valve, but the cold, unforgiving ice blocked the oxygen's passage.

It is so cold. How high have I climbed? Why am I here?

I cannot remember.

Tap the panel.

Why?

I do not know. It is just that one must tap the panel.

I will tap it, near the clock.

See the clock?

Does the little boy know how to tell time?

Yes, mama. When the big hand is on the twelve and the little hand is on the five, I will come home for dinner.

You are a good boy, Anton.

There is terrible cold all around me.

Mama, I am frightened.

Almost six miles in the sky, the slender sailplane turned slowly on one wing until the wind was behind it and then, as if it had a purpose of its own, it lowered its nose and dove for a short distance. The nose came up gently, the plane slowed, sank through the air, then dipped its nose again and began the cycle over again, porpoising its way down through the freezing air toward the sunlight in the valley far below.

11

"How do you like that?" asked Bill Webster. He had just put the Schweizer 2-32 through a combination loop and snap roll.

"Not bad," said Barney Fields. "I don't think this plane is stressed for that kind of stunt, though."

"You're a cool sonofabitch," said Webster.

"Maybe," said Barney, crossing his controls and putting the sailplane into a flat spin. "Get out of this one."

"Get out of it yourself."

The plane spun toward the green and yellow fields below. Neither man reached for the controls.

Webster cursed and shoved the plane's nose down, then recovered from the spin. He turned the ship toward the mountain range.

"We may not make it back to the field," he said. "There's quite a wind."

"That's your problem," said Barney. "Of course, you realize that all of your stunting around up here has put us so far off course that nobody back at Eielson has the faintest idea where we are."

"Radio them."

"Radio's out, remember?"

"I thought that was just something you said."

Barney smiled. "You thought wrong. It really did go out."

"Well, what do you suggest?"

"Not a damned thing," said Barney. "It wasn't my idea to

go flying this afternoon anyway. You got us up here, you get us down."

"If you'd opened your goddamned mouth, we wouldn't be downwind of the field," said Webster.

"You were too busy trying to outfly me to listen," Barney said. "You made a big point of taking charge of this aircraft. If you wanted my help, you should have asked for it. You're either in command or you're not. It isn't a committee operation. Now, if you want me to take over and fly us out of this pretty pickle you've screwed us into, I'll be glad to oblige."

"The hell with you!" yelled Webster. "If that's the way you want it, just keep your advice to yourself. I'll get us out of here without any fancy help from you. Don't worry about your plane. If I crack her up, I'll buy you another one. Just keep your goddamned lip buttoned."

"Consider it buttoned," Barney said grimly. "Now let's see what kind of man you really are, Mr. Mayor."

Webster swore under his breath as he hauled the sailplane up into another thermal and watched the altimeter crawl up to eleven thousand feet. He turned into the wind and tried to make a dash across the valley, but the airspeed indicator crept up toward the red line and his ground track did little more than hold its own. He was forced to turn away from the wind again, toward the mountains which were getting very close now.

The twin peaks of Mount Deborah and Mount Hayes were both higher than the straining sailplane, but there was a pass between them and he seemed to have enough altitude to get through it. Once through, he woull be over the safety of the Tanana River Valley. *If* he could get through.

Webster glanced over his shoulder at Barney. The tall Texan sat with both eyes closed, his arms crossed on his chest.

Okay, you stubborn sonofabitch, Webster thought.

He lowered the plane's nose and aimed the ship at the mountain pass. No sooner had both walls folded around the plane than the lift vanished and Webster saw, with anxiety, that the red pellet was high in its tube. The snow below came closer and closer. He knew, with a sinking feeling in his stomach, that he no longer had enough altitude to get through the pass.

At the last moment, he hauled back on the stick and tried that impossibility in a glider, a climbing turn.

The Schweizer 2-32 rose a few feet as the wings came around, and then all airspeed dropped away and Webster knew the ship was in a stall.

Get that nose down, fast!

But as he did, he saw that they were falling onto a ridge, several hundred feet up the sheer side of the mountain. Desperately, he flared out his glide and managed to slide onto a small flat area of snow. He jammed the stick forward and the sailplane stood on its nose, then fell back with a solid thump.

Barney Fields raised the canopy, unbuckled his harness, stood on the seat and looked around with a low whistle.

"Congratulations, Webster," he said. "You've managed to land us on the goddamned side of Mount Deborah."

12

Both sailplanes were reported missing before 5:00 P.M. Suslov's when he had been out of radio contact for more than an hour, the two-place Schweizer when its tow pilot became worried after two hours of searching had brought no sight of it.

"I'm checking the Air Force radar plane," said Ron Smith. "Barney wasn't carrying a transponder in his Schweizer, but Suslov was. They ought to be able to pinpoint him for us."

Staff Sergeant Alvin Handley in the radar ship was most helpful.

"Yes sir," he said over the radio link, "We've got the Russian on the scope. He's awful low, though. He must be going in for a landing. Right now, he's all the way over on the other side of the Talkeetna Mountains, down in the lake country. I'd put him just a mile or so from Lake Louise. There's a strip there, so that's where he might be headed."

"Good," said Smith. "His radio may be out of order. Do you by any chance have another blip on the scope, a sailplane without a transponder?"

"Sorry, sir," said Handley. "But, you know, there was something funny about that Russian a couple of hours back."

"What do you mean, funny?"

"Well, he was just downwind of Mount McKinley, and he kept getting brighter and brighter on the scope, so I knew he was climbing. Then, just as I was wondering how high he figured on going, his blip blinked out on me. But that's impossible. He would have had to climb higher than us for that to happen, and today we're circling at fifty-two thousand feet. I figured that his transponder must have cut out for a few minutes, because a little while later he was back on the screen and he's kept on his present course straight as an arrow ever since."

Smith was thanking the sergeant when the operations phone rang and Tim Sanders answered it. He spoke quietly for a moment and then hung up.

"Well," he said, "Suslov's plane just landed a half mile from the Lake Louise strip."

"That's good," said Smith.

"Not so good," Sanders said grimly. "The plane landed by itself. Suslov is dead."

JULY 8: *Discovery Day*

1

ALTHOUGH it was nearly 1:00 A.M., the sun was still high and this only seemed to emphasize the subdued quietness of the airbase. The usual raucousness of the traditional end-of-contest beer bust was missing, and Ron Smith's footsteps were loud and echoing as he and the governor of Alaska walked slowly down the runway. Major Anton Suslov's undamaged KAI-24 sat nearby, one wing down and weighted with a parachute.

"I'm sure Bill would want Discovery Day to go on," said the governor. "Too many people have come up here for us to cancel."

"Of course," said Ron Smith. "And the air show will go on as scheduled, too."

"We couldn't ask your fliers to do that."

"And they couldn't *not* do it. I talked things over with Suslov's team. They asked that he lie in state in the operations hangar for the rest of the day. They'll fly out around midnight. But they want to stay for the air show and fly in it."

"Can anyone tell what happened?"

"His barographs give us a good idea. One went right off the paper at fifty thousand feet. The other registered an ascent to 54,700, where the climb sloped off and a gradual descent began. We assume his altimeter froze up and he misjudged how high he really was. Somewhere up there, his lungs hemorrhaged and the ship flew itself to a safe landing. It must have been at least ninety below zero at the top of his climb. The plastic canopy just crystallized."

"What a terrible thing," said the governor. "So useless. The competition was over."

"Suslov wanted more than a number on the winner's sheet. He wanted that world's altitude record. And he got it."

"You mean he'll get it even though it killed him?"

"We have no way of knowing when he died. We know when he released, and we know how high he flew, and when and where he landed. The barographs confirm his altitude, just as they would if he were alive. I checked this out with representatives from other countries, and they all agree. We'll submit this new record to the FAI just as we would under normal conditions. And there's every reason to believe it will be accepted. Suslov finally achieved what he was trying for, an absolute altitude of 54,700 feet and an altitude gain of 52,200. It'll be a long time before anyone else comes close to those numbers. I personally plan to sponsor a motion prohibiting altitude attempts above forty thousand feet until we have some means of pressurizing the sailplane."

"Too bad we didn't have that yesterday."

"Too little and too late. That's the history of flying. We learn from tragedy. I talked to Paul Bikle earlier in the evening. He's all broken up . . . feels it's somehow his fault for going so close to the limits when he set the record Suslov was trying to beat. It's just a mess all the way. Everyone feels pretty bad."

The two men walked in silence for a moment, past the long rows of sailplanes.

"Why do they do it?" asked the governor. "Look at the score. One man dead. Two missing. Several injured. Four planes destroyed. All that time, that money, those lives. And for what? Some insignificant silver medal."

"No," said Ron Smith. "For reaching toward what exceeds our grasp."

2

The temperature on the mountain was dropping fast. The flight thermometer in the Schweizer 2-32 read two degrees below zero Farenheit. The sailplane had been turned around in the snow and now sat poised at the very edge of the cliff that dropped off for almost eight hundred feet straight down.

Barney had unpacked the survival kit, and now its radar target flew from an aluminum pole a few feet up the mountainside.

"They'll find us pretty soon," Webster said.

"I doubt it," said Barney Fields. "There hasn't been a single search plane over this area. I'd say they're concentrating their operation in the McKinley area, where we're supposed to be."

"Well, if you remember," snapped Webster, "I'm not just any bush pilot."

"Oh, sure," said Barney. "You're the mayor of Fairbanks. But if you want my opinion, even for a very important person like yourself, they'll still search hardest where the plane was supposed to be. And that's around seventy miles west of here."

"You're the original hardass!" said Webster. "I'm trying to cheer you up, and you stick your thumb in my eye."

"Why don't we just drop it, Webster? I'm trying to decide what to do next."

"What we do next is wait for the Air National Guard to arrive," said Bill Webster.

"Which I hate to admit, but they've just done," said Barney. "Look up there. That's an L-16 on the other side of the peak."

"The flares!" yelled Webster.

"He's still too far away. We'll wait until he comes down this way."

"Damn it!" said Webster. "I don't think you *want* to be rescued!" He scrambled in the survival kit, got one of the three flares, pulled its ignition ring, and watched a ball of flame arc into the sky. The brightness of the sun and the glare of the surrounding snow and ice made the flare almost invisible. "I thought it would be brighter," said Webster, reaching for another of the red tubes. Barney caught his arm.

"Take it easy," drawled the pilot. "I told you he was too damned far away and now you've gone and wasted a flare. Now we've got two. He's either got to be closer than that, or we've got to wait until twilight so they'll show up better."

"Don't put your hands on me," said Webster.

"Okay," said Barney, "but don't you go grabbing for any more of those flares or I'll be obliged to knock you on your Alaskan ass."

Webster was not listening. "The plane's gone," he said.

"There never was much chance he'd see us anyway," said Barney. "This is a white ship on white snow. They may not spot us even if they fly right over this valley. But if we're lucky and the light is right, and these two flares both work

. . . well, maybe they'll locate us before we freeze to death."

"And what then? They can't get a chopper in here. The cliffs are too close and the wind's too rough. Maybe they can drop supplies."

"Not a chance if this wind keeps up," said Barney. "They can't get over us from the side, because the wind and the cliff walls won't let them. And the top of this ridge is a good thousand feet overhead. The wind would blow any parachute way the hell off target before it could get down here."

"How did you last this long in flying?" Webster said bitterly. "I've never seen such a defeatist attitude."

"On the contrary," said Barney, "I'm not defeated at all. I don't doubt for a minute that we're going to get out of here. But nobody's going to rescue us. We're going to have to figure it out all on our lonesome. So why don't you crawl back in the cockpit where we can keep a little warm while we do some hard thinking."

Webster cursed under his breath, but he got into the sailplane and huddled against Barney Fields for warmth.

3

A military honor guard stood at the four corners of the dull bronze casket supported on trestles in the rear of the operations hangar. It was now 8:00 A.M. and small groups of pilots and crewmen came to look down at Major Anton Suslov. The Russian was dressed in a fresh green flight suit. The fliers moved slowly, spoke in low voices, and shook their heads as they passed.

"Poor bastard," said Chet Cameron as he left the hangar.

"He's got his blasted record now. For what good it'll do him."

The winding line of silent men was joined by one woman.

Renée Duval, in her flight suit, stood at the casket for a long moment. Impulsively, she reached out and touched his cheek. But it was not flesh any longer; merely cold, hard wax.

She swayed for a brief second, then recovered herself and left the hangar. Outside, in the cool morning breeze, she looked up at the cumulus forming in the sky, and when her voice came it was no more than a whisper.

"Oh, my God, my God . . . I loved him and he never knew it."

4

The Communications Center of Eielson Air Force Base was a madhouse. Captain Tim Sanders held one of a pair of earphones up to his head, listening and speaking into a hand microphone.

"Have your planes widened their search to take in the easterly mountains?" asked Ron Smith. "All I can figure is that they may have been blown off their course and never got down to the McKinley area at all."

"Since sunup," said Sanders. He pressed the earphones tighter and broke out in a grin. "Hot damn!" he said. "We've spotted them. They piled up on a mountain ledge on the southeast side of Mount Deborah."

"Are they all right?" Smith asked anxiously.

"The L-16 couldn't get too close. The winds are murder. But the pilot saw two men jumping up and down, so aside from a slight case of frostbite, they should be all right."

"How did your men spot them?"

"The radar plane picked up a small target that just sat in one place. They must have had one of our survival kits aboard and used the radar flag. Anyway, we sent in the L-16, and there they were. Now that we've found them, all we have to figure out is how to get them down."

"That ought to be easy," said Smith.

5

"Like hell it'll be easy," Barney told Bill Webster. "Did you see what happened to that L-16 when he tried to get in close? He damned near wiped himself out against the face of the cliff."

"Here comes a helicopter," said Webster. "Maybe he'll have better luck."

But the big chopper was unable to get closer than a thousand feet out over the valley. The stranded men saw the white plume of a parachute open as a bundle was tipped over the edge of the loading hatch, but the wind caught the nylon and whipped the parachute away from the ledge at a fantastic speed.

Another hour passed and then they heard the whine of a jet.

"Here comes the heavy stuff," said Barney.

A Starfire jet swept into view, boring its way through the wind, but rocking from side to side in the fierce turbulence.

"Watch your head!" yelled Barney. "I think he's going to try to dive bomb us."

The Starfire made a wide turn out into the valley, then aimed directly at the tiny ledge and streaked toward it.

Half a mile out, the pilot pulled up into a vertical climb and a black object left the bottom of the plane and curved through the air toward the ledge. As it tumbled toward them, they saw it was a droppable gasoline tank.

"That's going to come pretty close," muttered Webster.

"He aimed behind us," said Barney. "It won't hit the Schweizer."

The wing tank struck the snowbank fifty yards above their position, burst open, and threw coils of rope and climbing equipment out over the snow. Before they could rush for the gear, the cliffside gave a monstrous cough and avalanched down the slope, carrying tons of ice and stone—and all the supplies—over the edge of the cliff just yards behind the tail of the sailplane.

"Well," said Barney Fields, "back to the old drawing board. That's the last time they'll try that."

6

The three Russian sailplanes flew over the crowd at Fairbanks International in a broken diamond formation with the empty slot left for their fallen leader. Then, as one, they made a sweeping turn and landed.

The crowd was large, but respectfully quiet. They found the sailplanes fascinating, but the recent tragedy had touched them all.

As for the pilots themselves, the news that Barney Fields and Bill Webster had been found safe, although trapped on a ledge, brightened the day a bit. Amanda Webster hired a light plane to fly her into the valley, while Ron Smith began examining plans for an aerotow to snatch the fallen Schweizer from the mountain. As more accurate descriptions of the terrain and winds came in, he abandoned his plan.

"To be honest," said Tim Sanders, "I don't think we're going to be able to reach them. So far, we haven't even been able to drop them a coil of rope. The situation is fantastic. I think all we're going to be able to do is lend moral support. We have a team of mountain climbers at the base of the cliff, but though they'll keep trying, their opinion is that it's unclimbable."

"Well, this is ridiculous," said Ron Smith. "Do you mean to say that we have them in sight and can't reach them? I never heard of such a thing."

"Mr. Smith," said the retrieve officer, "this is Alaska. There's a lot of things up here most folks haven't heard of."

7

"What are those crazy bastards up to now?" asked Barney Fields.

"I can't tell," said Bill Webster. His face was severely sunburned, and he had smeared ointment from the survival kit along his cheekbones and down the bridge of his nose, and the effect was to make him look like a pale Indian.

The L-16 shuddered to within a thousand feet or so, almost overhead, dangerously close to the face of the cliff. The plane bounced, and a dark object hurtled from it.

"Sonofabitch!" said Barney. "That's a *man*!"

It was. A daring parachutist, wearing the latest in steerable parachutes, the two-strip "flying chute," also known as the "Flying Band-aid." The chutist let himself drop for almost five hundred feet before pulling the rip cord. As they heard the distant *snap* of the air filling the parachute, the man was swept almost over them.

"The nutty bastard might just make it," yelled Barney. "Get ready to give him a hand!"

The parachutist was only yards above them now, but floating toward the dropoff rapidly. He was laden down with heavy bags of equipment hanging from both legs.

"Grab hold of him!" Barney called. "He's going over!"

They managed to catch one of the duffel bags and tried to prevent the skydiver from being pulled over the edge of the cliff, but the wind caught the parachute and their dug-in heels were scraped toward the abyss.

"Hang onto the duffel bag!" yelled the parachutist. He drew a knife and slashed at its rope. As it parted, the two pilots fell back into the snow, clutching the bag. The chutist was swept out over the valley by the howling wind. They watched anxiously as he nearly collapsed his parachute. Then he regained control and was carried out of sight down into the valley.

"Where do they find guys like that?" Barney said softly.

"Let's see what's in the bag," said Webster.

But the contents were disappointing. Although there was food and water, apparently the bulk of the nylon ropes had been distributed in other bags. The two hundred feet of rope they found was not nearly long enough to reach the safety of the valley floor.

"Maybe we could pop our chute open and cut up the shroud lines to make a rope," Webster said.

"Wouldn't work," said Barney. "Not long enough and too thin to climb down even if it were. But wait just a damned minute. You gave me an idea."

"What?"

"The parachutes. They just might do it."

"Do what?"

"We're through waiting for the Air National Guard to save us," said Barney Fields. "Now it's our turn to show some action."

"Such as?" asked Bill Webster.

"We're going to fly this sailplane right off this lousy mountain," said Barney Fields.

8

Renée Duval reached Fairbanks International at five thousand feet. The flight from Eielson had been made in a daze. Her suddenly-realized loss had left a terrible blade of pain in her mind, and she flew mechanically, without joy. She had promised the air show committee an aerobatic show, and she would deliver, but then she must go back to that silent hangar and the man who slept there.

She dove for speed and put the Edelweiss through a beautiful inside loop. The crowd far below "ahhhed" and she decided to show them a spin. The sailplane's nose came up and slowed, then turned as she threw in hard rudder and began the spin. The earth below looked like a whirling phonograph record. Renée counted three complete revolutions as the Edelweiss spun toward the airfield below. Time to come out of it, she thought, as she put in opposite rudder. She felt the spin start to slow, then she applied forward stick pressure.

The spin seemed to stop, but then it continued through the

center and started in the other direction. The nose of the Edelweiss would not come down!

The gear in the back! thought Renée. The ship is so tail-heavy that I can't pull her nose down!

"Something's wrong up there," muttered Chet Cameron.

As the spin continued, Renée threw off her harness and tried to reach back into the storage compartment to pull some of the equipment further forward. But the excess G-forces threw her up against the outside of the spinning plane, and she knew that there was no possible way to save the Edelweiss.

Renée released the canopy lock and pushed the plastic up and away from her. The wind caught it and threw it back, away from the wildly spinning ship. Now the shrieking wind rushed in and tore at her body. She reached for the rip cord, gripped it, and leaped over the side of the cockpit.

Released from her weight, the Edelweiss reared and bucked and the low wing smashed into the girl, literally scooped her up, and flung her back into the cockpit. She landed with a bone-jarring impact and sat there, numbed, before realizing that she had to leap out of the ship on the inside of the spin, not the outside. She saw the ground coming up closer. Frightened, she dove over the edge of the cockpit again and this time she fell clear of the sailplane. Then another pang of fear shot through her.

She could not find the rip cord!

"Open," whispered Wolf Lindner, standing near his just-landed Ka-20. "Make it open, God!"

The crowd screamed as the black dot fell nearer, becoming a human figure with arms and legs that flailed at the air as if she were trying to swim through its emptiness. Then the nylon canopy flowered out above the plunging body and snapped open fully just before she struck the grass at the runway's edge. The parachute dragged her fifty yards before Chet Cameron ran over to collapse it.

"Is she all right?" he gasped, running back down the shroud lines.

"Nothing seems broken," said Wolf Lindner. "But, my God, look at her chest!"

In her last spasms of animal fear, as she fell toward the earth, unable to find the rip cord, Renée had clawed through her flight suit, through the blouse underneath, and the soft flesh, right down to the naked whiteness of bone.

Renée opened her eyes and looked at Chet. "Anton," she whispered. "He is gone. I want to die." Then she fainted.

As the ambulance took her away, Wolf shook his head, his lips tight.

"Perhaps her mind wanted to die," he said. "But the animal within would have clawed her to bloody ribbons to save itself."

And he wondered if there was such an animal inside *him*. He hoped not, but he was afraid there was.

9

"You're out of your skull," said Bill Webster. "I won't go along with such a hare-brained idea."

"You don't have any choice," said Barney. "We sure in hell aren't going to sit here and watch some other skydiver bash his brains out trying to save our asses. Now, get in that plane and hang on."

"Shove it," said Webster.

"Okay," said Barney, giving Webster a cracking punch

against the point of the jaw. Webster went down to one knee.

"You hit me," he said numbly, a thin trickle of blood running down from where he had bitten his own lip.

"And I'll hit you again," Barney promised grimly, "if you don't get your ass in that sailplane."

Webster looked at him hard, saw no bluff in Barney's eyes, and got up slowly. He crawled into the rear seat and strapped himself in. The plastic canopy had been removed and now lay to one side. Barney had tied one end of the coil of rope to the front tow hook of the sailplane and the other end to the harness of his·parachute.

He climbed into the front seat of the Schweizer, holding the parachute.

"Okay, he said, "now if you're not too pissed off at me to help out, I'd suggest you get your feet on the rudder pedals and grab hold of the stick with one hand. Hang onto the cable release with the other hand. If this works, we're going to get yanked off here so hard it'll probably be all I can do to keep from falling out. You'll have to fly her for a while until I get settled."

"Don't worry about me," said Webster. "I just hope your screwy idea works."

"Even if it doesn't," said Barney, "how could we be any worse off? I'll give you a deal, if we make it you get one free poke at my jaw." He hefted the parachute. "Ready?"

"Any time," said Webster.

Barney pulled the rip cord and the spring-powered drogue chute popped out. Cradling the parachute in one arm like a huge football, he heaved it out as far as he could. For an awful second, the canvas packet seemed to fall lifelessly through the air. At the very last moment, the wind caught the small drogue chute, pulled it out and away from the main bundle, and the larger canopy followed it out. The rope burned through Barney's hands as he played the billowing parachute like a huge sailfish. As the parachute blossomed, the rope was almost taut.

"Get ready!" yelled Barney. The rope ripped out of his hands and with a savage, sickening thumping noise, the sailplane was literally snatched off the ridge by the rope attached to the parachute.

Barney was thrown back into the cockpit. His head struck one side, and he collapsed forward, nearly falling from the sailplane.

Webster pulled the red release knob and banked the plane toward the angry teeth of the rocks. Barney fell back into his seat, and Webster turned the plane away. The parachute still yanked on the tow hook, but then it released and Bill Webster turned the Schweizer toward the valley floor below.

10

"I guess I owe you one free poke," said Barney Fields. "So go ahead and take your best shot."

Amanda stood near the sailplane, watching them.

"Let's call it even," said Bill Webster. He looked over at his wife. "I guess you heard. Barney saved my life, after I made a fool of myself."

"I heard," she told him.

"Well?"

"You're not the only one who can make a fool of himself," she said. She went over to Barney and kissed his cheek. "Barney, forgive me. I guess I had the seven-year-itch."

"Sure," he said. "Take care of him, will you? He's a good man."

"So are you," she said.

She took her husband's arm and they walked together to one of two waiting L-16s.

When the first L-16 was off the ground, Barney helped hook up to the second.

"Where to?" asked the tow pilot.

"Do you think you can make Texas?" asked Barney Fields.

"Huh?"

Barney smiled. "Forget it," he said. "I'll get there on my own."

Confessions from the Author

ALTHOUGH *The Green Air* is fiction and none of the characters in it exist anywhere except in my imagination, I must offer apologies to the real people who have either been mentioned or who have been erased from my fictional history of an international soaring meet.

I hope that veteran sailplane pilot Richard E. Schreder will forgive me for breaking his leg, but I had to keep Dick out of the Championships, or my own imaginary pilots would not have had a chance. The same goes for Wally Scott, and perhaps twenty other American pilots, any one of whom could have flown rings around Barney Fields. I had to pretend they were unavailable for the U.S. team, otherwise their genuine exploits would have made my fictional hero look sick.

Too many people have helped in the creation of this novel to allow a complete listing, but certainly the cooperation of the folks at Alaska Airways made my job easier. Gratitude goes to Bob Wilcox of the U.S. Air Force Reserve for helping with the flight plans that were so necessary for my fictional adventures.

Special thanks, too, to Paul F. Bikle, who set the real sailplane altitude record of 46,267 feet flying a Schweizer 1-23E on February 25, 1961, in the Bishop, California, wave. And to Soviet pilot Mikhail Vierietiennikov who made the world's longest flight to a predetermined point on June 18, 1960, from Orechkovo to Ravkoska, Russia, flying an A-15 sailplane a distance of almost 444 miles. Also to Alvin Parker of Odessa, Texas, who flew a Nemi SISU sailplane 646 miles for the distance record. Their achievements were truly won, and I beg many pardons for exceeding them in the name of fiction.

I recognize that by the time this novel is published, new records may exist, and to their holders, a tip of my typewriter.

Some of the books and publications I found helpful in the preparation of this novel include *This Is Alaska*, by Harry Kursh, published by Prentice-Hall; *Soaring Guide*, by Peter M. Bowers, one of the Modern Aircraft series; *On Being a Bird*, by Philip Wills, published by Sailflying Press Ltd. of London; *Soaring for Diamonds*, by Joseph Colville Lincoln, published by the Northland Press of Flagstaff, Arizona; *Where No Birds Fly*, by Philip Wills, published by Newnes of London; *Youth Must Fly*, published by Harper and Brothers; *The Soaring Pilot*, by Ann and Lorne Welch and F. G. Irving, published by John Murray of London; and, of course, the delightful magazine of American sailplaning, *Soaring, The Journal Of The Soaring Society of America*, P.O. Box 66071, Los Angeles, California.

Many of my soaring companions read the mansucript for accuracy, including Paul Schweizer of the Schweizer Aircraft Company, Elmira, New York, but any errors of fact or opinion remaining are mine, not theirs.